TAMING THE ROGUE

BWWM HISTORICAL ROMANCE

SAGE DEARLY

TAMING THE ROGUE

CHAPTER-1

The bar was a pit, a place where desperation and sweat clung to the walls and every glance was a threat or a deal waiting to happen. For a woman like her, it was a good place to disappear.

She wasn't here for pleasure, though, and she moved through the crowd with purpose, her eyes skimming over faces, looking for anything that would get her through the night.

A quick swipe of a coin purse, a scrap of food, whatever she could find. Then that very night, her gaze settled on something far more tempting.

The man sitting in the corner had an elegant air about him. He didn't belong there, not with that tailored jacket, the way his fingers lazily toyed with a glass of expensive bourbon.

His henchmen sat close by, broad-shouldered, cold-eyed men who looked like they'd slit a throat just as soon as they'd shake a hand. But it wasn't them that held her attention.

It was him.

He was watching her, though he tried to make it seem casual. His eyes, a sharp blue that cut through the smoky room, had followed her movements ever since she walked in. It wasn't the first time she'd been stared at in this place.

Men looked at her all the time, most of them hoping for something they would not get. There was something different about this one, primarily because his gaze wasn't filled with lust or hunger. It was more curiosity than anything, like he was trying to figure her out.

She felt it immediately, that spark of danger. Men like him weren't safe because they didn't need to steal or swindle to get what they wanted; they could take it.

Something about his cool confidence tugged at her and she ignored the heat rising from her neck and turned away, pretending not to notice. He was just another rich man, simply another fool.

No matter how hard she tried, her mind kept drifting back to him. His silence unnerved her. He had made no moves, hadn't said a word to anyone since he arrived, and that was odd.

Men like him usually barked orders, threw money around, and expected the world to obey. He was waiting. For what, she couldn't tell.

Shaking the feeling off, she focused on the job. She

slid between tables with the ease of someone who had lived their whole life dodging trouble. A quick swipe here, a slip of her hand there, and she'd already made off with a few coins from a drunkard passed out by the bar.

Her eyes flicked back to the man in the corner. The way he watched her, and it was almost as if he knew what she was doing. She clenched her jaw, feeling a flicker of irritation. Let him watch. Let him think whatever he wanted. He was still just a mark.

She bided her time, moving closer with each pass, her fingers itching for that wallet she could see peeking out of his coat. He didn't need it, not like she did.

A man like him had probably never missed a meal in his life. She, on the other hand, hadn't eaten more than scraps in days.

As she neared him again, her heart raced within her chest, the pounding becoming almost deafening, and with a newfound courage, she deliberately brushed just a little closer to him this time.

She could smell the rich leather of his jacket, the faint scent of something expensive clinging to him. Her fingers flexed at her side, waiting for the perfect moment.

As she extended her hand to grab his wallet, a moment of doubt caused her to hesitate. He hadn't moved an inch, but his eyes met hers, as if he had been waiting for this exact moment. There was a challenge in his gaze, daring her to go through with it.

Her throat tightened, but she refused to back down. She was no coward, and she sure as hell wasn't about to let some fancy man scare her off.

With a quick movement, her hand slipped inside his coat, but before she could grab the wallet, his powerful hand clamped down on her wrist.

The room seemed to still as his grip tightened, not enough to hurt, but enough to make it clear she wasn't going anywhere. Her heart raced, and for the first time in a long while, she felt a flicker of fear.

"You've been busy tonight," he said, his voice low and smooth, as if they were the only two people in the room. He didn't look angry. Amused, maybe. Intrigued.

She jerked her hand, trying to free herself, but his grip didn't budge. "Let go of me," she spat, her voice sharp, raw. "I didn't take nothin'."

"No," he said calmly, his eyes still holding hers. "Not yet."

"Thought you could just take from me, huh?" he continued, and even though his voice wasn't raised, there was power in it. Command.

Her heart pounded against her ribs, but she masked it with defiance, jerking her arm back. "Ain't worth what you think you are," she spat, yanking hard.

She wasn't scared, she couldn't afford to be, but her pulse hammered in her ears. Stupid. She'd been stupid to think she could outsmart him.

The henchmen circled her now, eyes dark with intent. One of them cracked his knuckles, stepping in too close. "Maybe we should teach her some manners."

A hard knot formed in her gut. She knew how this went. This wasn't the first time she'd been cornered. She braced herself, body tense, but the rich man held up a hand, and, just like that, they stopped.

He rose slowly, his eyes cold, scrutinizing her as if she were nothing more than an animal caught in a trap. "What's your name?"

Her lips twisted into a sneer. "Ain't got one."

He tilted his head, amused. "Everyone's got a name."

"I said, I ain't got one," she snapped, voice raw, edged with years of survival. She wasn't giving him anything, not a damn thing.

The man took a slow step closer, his gaze pinning her where she stood. The space that separated them was thick with an electrifying and uneasy atmosphere. "You're either brave or foolish."

"Maybe I'm both." She held his stare, defiance flickering in her eyes like a wild flame. She wouldn't let him see the fear creeping up her spine.

The henchman from earlier growled low, "Let me handle her, boss."

For a second, she thought he might. She could feel the threat hanging thick between them, the promise of violence hovering just beneath the surface. Her mouth dried up, heart racing. She stood tall and refused to cower.

Instead of giving the order, the man's lips curled in

a slow, bitter smile. "No." His eyes flicked back to her. "She'll pay for her mistake another way." He motioned to his men. "Take her to the estate."

Her stomach dropped. The estate? What did he mean by that? She fought the urge to bolt, but knew they'd catch her in seconds if she tried. She cursed under her breath. Damn it. Why had she made such a stupid mistake?

They grabbed her, none too gently, dragging her out into the night. The feeling that she had gone from one type of trap to another was certain.

CHAPTER-2

*T*he frosty night air hit her like a slap as they dragged her out of the bar. Her feet stumbled over the uneven ground, but the men holding her didn't care.

Their grips were tight, unyielding, and she could feel the bruises forming under their fingers. She cursed herself for getting caught, for letting him get inside her head.

She glanced up, just for a second, and saw him walking ahead of them, his steps slow, unhurried. He didn't seem the least bit bothered by what was happening.

Like this was routine for him, dragging women out of bars and into the unknown. The fear that had been creeping up her spine since he grabbed her wrist was now a steady throb in the pit of her stomach.

They reached his carriage, a sleek, dark thing that

looked out of place in the grimy street. One henchman yanked open the door, shoving her forward. She twisted, trying to pull away, but it was useless.

"Get in," he ordered, voice flat.

Her teeth gritted in response, and she considered making a run for it, but where could she go? They'd hunt her down before she even reached the edge of town. Swallowing her pride, she glared at him. "What's this, huh? You get your kicks takin' girls like me to your fancy house? I ain't gonna play the part."

He met her gaze, unmoved by her words. "You'll do as I say, or you won't like the alternative."

The way he said it, calm, with that chilling authority, made her blood run cold. She clenched her fists, her whole body rigid with defiance. With no other choice, she climbed into the carriage. She'd been cornered before, but never like this.

Inside, it was silent, and the quiet made her skin prickle. He sat across from her, his eyes still on her as if he were studying her, like she was some kind of puzzle. She hated it, and she hated him.

Under that hate, however, there was something else, something that made her feel heat in her very core. It made her feel small and vulnerable in the vastness of that carriage, in the presence of this man who had all the power, while she had none.

"You're quiet," he said after a moment. His voice was smooth, not mocking, but she could hear the amusement in it.

"What you expect me to say?" she snapped, crossing her arms. "You think I'm gonna thank you for dragging me out of there?"

His lips curled into the smallest of smiles. "No. I don't expect gratitude."

"Good," she shot back, though the anger in her voice masked the tremor in her chest. She wasn't used to feeling this helpless, this trapped. Every part of her screamed to fight, to claw her way out, but she was outnumbered, outmaneuvered. For now.

The road outside blurred into the night as the carriage rattled over uneven ground, pulling them away from the bar and deeper into his world.

She didn't like the quiet, didn't enjoy being left with nothing but her thoughts and the heavy weight of his gaze.

"So, what's the plan?" she finally asked, her voice thick with sarcasm. "You gonna keep me as some kind of prisoner? Or is this where you throw me into one of those fancy dungeons I heard rich folks got?"

"I don't have a dungeon," he replied, his tone so calm it was infuriating.

"Then what do you want from me?" Her voice rose with the question, sharp and desperate. She didn't care if he heard the fear now. It was spilling out of her in jagged pieces, and she couldn't stop it.

He didn't answer right away. Instead, he leaned back, eyes never leaving her. "You tried to take what was mine," he said, each word slow, deliberate. "And now, you'll repay me."

"Repay you?" She barked out a bitter laugh. "I got nothin'. You know that, besides, I stole nothing."

"You'll work it off," he said simply. "As my maid."

Her mouth fell open, and for a moment, all the words in her head tangled together in a mess of disbelief and rage. "Your maid?" she echoed, incredulous. "You think I'm gonna scrub your floors, serve you drinks like I'm some servant?"

"That's exactly what you'll do." He tilted his head slightly, eyes narrowing just enough to show his patience was wearing thin. "Unless you'd prefer a different fate."

She opened her mouth to hurl another insult, but the way he looked at her, the quiet threat in his eyes, made her close it just as fast. This wasn't a game. He wasn't bluffing.

"You ain't got the right," she muttered, though her voice had lost some of its fire.

"I have every right," he said. "You took from me. Now, you owe me."

She wanted to spit at him, to tell him where he could shove his threats, but the truth was sinking in. He had her and there was nothing she could do about it.

To the world, her opinions and desires were overlooked, leaving her with no say. That she had black skin meant that she was considered being without power, enabling him to have complete control over her. Hell, if he had called the police, she would be worse off.

The carriage came to a stop, and when the door swung open, she felt the chill of the night air hit her again.

The estate loomed ahead, dark, sprawling, and foreign. It wasn't a place for someone like her. She didn't belong there, but there she was, and if she liked it or not, she would have to play his game.

CHAPTER-3

The atmosphere in the estate was overwhelming and suffocating.

She had thought the carriage ride was the worst of it, but stepping inside his home was like entering a world that wasn't meant for her.

The walls were too pristine, the air too still, like it was holding its breath, waiting for her to break something.

Her footsteps echoed in the grand hall as if announcing how out of place she was. But she would not let that bother her, not in front of him.

He walked ahead, not bothering to glance back, trusting his henchmen to keep her in line. She trailed behind, her wrists still sore from their grip, but her spirit was far from broken. She wasn't about to play the obedient little servant, no matter how many threats he threw her way.

They stopped in front of a large wooden door. Without a word, one of his men opened it, revealing a dimly lit room with a narrow bed, a washbasin, and little else. A maid's quarters, which were to be her new prison.

"This is where you'll stay," he said, finally turning to face her. His expression was unreadable, like he didn't care whether she screamed or surrendered.

She crossed her arms, raising her chin defiantly. "It's better than the streets," she muttered, though there was a bitterness in her tone. She would not thank him for this. He'd only dragged her out of one hell and thrown her into another.

"It's clean," he said simply. "You'll start work at dawn."

She scoffed. "And what exactly do you think I'm gonna do here? Dust your fancy bookshelves? Wash your silk sheets?" She spewed the words like they were poison. "I ain't never cleaned for nobody in my life, and I sure as hell ain't gonna start now."

His gaze hardened, and for the first time since they met, a flicker of something dark crossed his face. "You'll learn," he hissed, his voice low but firm. "You don't have a choice."

Her jaw clenched, and she fought the urge to snap back. Every muscle in her body screamed for her to fight, to lash out, to tear down this illusion of control he had over her. There was a small part of her also, a part she hated, that knew he was right. She had no other options.

Instead of answering, she turned her back on him and stalked into the room, slamming the door shut behind her. She leaned against it, letting out a shaky breath, her heart pounding in her chest. She wouldn't let him see her break.

As she entered the small room, she closed the door with a sigh, leaning her back against the wood, her mind heavy with thoughts.

Life had not been kind. From birth on a plantation, she had been a ghost in the world, evading capture and slipping through the cracks of society since she escaped the suffocating chains of servitude.

She had survived on wit and grit, refusing to bend to anyone's will. She'd learned to pick pockets, charm her way out of danger, and even slip unnoticed into houses of ill repute, doing whatever it took to stay one step ahead of the law or anyone who might seek to claim her.

As she grew older and her body matured, her curves became another tool, a dangerous one. Her once lanky frame blossomed into voluptuous hips, full breasts, and thighs that caught the eye of every man she passed. It wasn't long before men started looking at her in ways she didn't welcome.

Unwanted hands had grazed her more than once, and their affection, masked as desire, was something she learned to flee from with practiced ease.

Despite the leering eyes and whispered offers, she remained untouched, pure, not by innocence but by sheer will. She had perfected the art of flirtation, of making a man believe she might offer more, giving nothing at all.

Her ebony skin glistened in the candlelight, and she glimpsed herself in the dusty mirror that hung on the far wall. The brown eyes, soulful and wise beyond their years, held secrets and stories no one knew.

With their full and inviting appearance, her lips had the power to draw in many men, who were ultimately left unsatisfied.

Her curves, those same hips that had earned her attention both wanted and unwanted, felt like both a blessing and a curse, something that protected her yet made her vulnerable all at once.

What set her apart was her remarkable skill in finding a delicate balance between persevering against all odds and knowing when to let go.

She had made it this far without losing herself. With this rich man watching her every move in the horrible place, she was determined not to falter. The process of her falling asleep was dragged out because he continuously intruded upon her dreams.

The sun had barely risen when she was woken by a loud knock on the door. She ignored it at first, pulling the thin blanket over her head, but the knock came again, more insistent this time.

"Up," came a gruff voice from the other side of the door. "Master's orders."

She rolled her eyes, her anger simmering just beneath the surface. "Master's orders," she muttered to herself, throwing the blanket aside and swinging her legs out of bed. She would not make this easy for him.

The door creaked open, and one servant, a woman, stern-faced and brisk, stood there, holding out a plain, gray dress. "Put this on," the woman said without a hint of emotion. "You're expected downstairs in ten minutes."

She snatched the dress from her hands, holding it like it was something vile. "I ain't wearin' this," she said, her voice sharp.

"You will, or you'll answer to him." The woman's

eyes flicked to her face, cold and unsympathetic. "He doesn't like to be kept waiting."

The door shut before she could argue, leaving her alone with the dress in her hands.

Her fingers tightened around the rough fabric, her chest burning with frustration. She wanted to rip it to shreds, to toss it out the window and scream at the absurdity of it all. Instead, she gritted her teeth and pulled the dress over her head.

She looked at herself in the small, cracked mirror by the washbasin. The woman staring back wasn't the same one who had strutted into the bar the night before. This one looked... smaller.

Trapped, but her eyes still held that fire, that defiance. She wasn't beaten. Not yet.

When she entered the dining room, he was already there, seated at the head of the long, polished table. He didn't look up as she approached, casually cutting into a plate of food that looked far too rich for someone like her.

His silence was deafening, and for a moment, she was tempted to throw the plate at the wall, just to get some reaction out of him.

Instead, she walked to the far end of the room, her footsteps purposefully loud on the marble floor. He finally glanced up, his eyes sweeping over her in that infuriatingly calm way, as if measuring her.

"You're late," he said, his voice cutting through the silence.

She crossed her arms, her jaw set. "I ain't a maid," she shot back. "And I sure as hell ain't used to takin' orders."

"You'll get used to it." His tone was as smooth as the fine wine he was sipping, and it only made her angrier.

"You think you can tame me, don't you?" she challenged, her voice rising. "You think just 'cause you got money and power, you can make me do whatever you want?"

He didn't answer right away, just stared at her with that same maddening calm. Then he leaned forward slightly, his eyes narrowing. "You're here because you have no other choice. And whether you like it or not, you're under my roof now. You'll learn your place."

Her blood boiled at his words, but before she could spit out a retort, one of the other servants entered the room, cutting off the tension between them.

The moment was lost, but the fire in her chest burned hotter than ever.

CHAPTER-4

*C*ommands were given at the beginning of the day to set the tone.

Everywhere she turned, there was an order barked at her by some servant or staff member, each expecting her to fall in line like the rest of them.

The estate was a maze of polished wood and gleaming surfaces, and they wanted her to scrub and shine and polish it until she could see her reflection in every inch of the place. She wasn't having it.

Her hands ached from the rough bristles of the broom, the repetitive motion making her arm muscles burn. She swept the halls as instructed, but not without grumbling under her breath and making sure her scowl was visible to anyone who dared to glance her way.

They wouldn't see her break. No one would.

She paused for a moment, wiping her forehead with

the back of her hand and glaring at the spotless floor. The house was too damn clean.

She wasn't made for this. She could feel herself suffocating from the restrictions and control.

"You missed a spot."

His voice drifted from behind her, smooth as ever, and her spine straightened at the sound of it. She didn't turn around. Didn't acknowledge him.

"Wasn't aware I was supposed to be perfect," she muttered, her fingers tightening around the broom handle.

Despite not receiving an immediate response from him, she could sense his penetrating gaze fixed upon her back, observing her every move and patiently awaiting her reaction.

After a few agonizing seconds, he finally spoke, his tone softer than she expected. "Perfection isn't required. But obedience is."

The words crawled under her skin, making her blood boil. She turned to face him, fire in her eyes, her chin lifted in defiance. "I ain't your servant. You don't own me."

He raised an eyebrow, a flicker of amusement playing on his lips. "No, but you're here to work off your debt, remember? It's here or I hand you over to the Sheriff and you'll do what's required of you. Or do you want to add more to what you owe?"

She clenched her teeth, her hands itching to throw the broom down and storm out of the house. But where would she go? She was trapped, and he knew it. The bastard knew it.

"You don't scare me," she said, her voice low, dangerous.

"I don't need to scare you," he replied, stepping closer, his presence looming over her. "I just need you to do your job."

Her heart pounded in her chest as he closed the distance between them. She hated how small she felt next to him, how his calm, composed demeanor only made her want to lash out more. She wanted to make him angry, to crack that perfect exterior and show that he wasn't in control.

But instead of reacting, he just stood there, waiting for her to make the next move.

The midday sun filtered through the windows as she found herself in the kitchen, peeling potatoes.

Her fingers moved automatically, the repetitive task dulling her senses. She hated this, the domesticity of it.

This wasn't who she was. She wasn't made for this kind of life.

Her thoughts were interrupted when the door swung open, and he entered, his steps measured. She didn't bother looking up, focusing instead on the knife in her hand as she peeled.

"You're still defiant," he observed, his voice cutting through the silence like a knife.

"And you're still a bastard," she shot back without missing a beat.

He approached, leaning against the counter opposite her, his eyes never leaving her face. "You've got a sharp tongue for someone who's in no position to speak freely."

She glanced up at him, her eyes narrowing. "I ain't in no position to do nothin'. You think just 'cause you're rich, you can bend people to your will. I've seen your kind before."

"And yet, you're still here," he replied, his tone almost conversational. "You're still under my roof, peeling my potatoes, like it or not."

Her hands tightened around the knife, wishing she could thrust it into his neck, frustration bubbling up inside her. "You don't know a damn thing about me."

"I know enough," he mumbled, his eyes boring into hers. "For instance, I know you're proud and know you've spent your life surviving. I also know you think you can fight me, resist me, but eventually, you'll realize there's no point."

She slammed the knife down on the counter, her chest heaving with anger. "You think I'll just roll over and obey you? Like I'm some kinda dog? I'll die before I let that happen."

He stared at her for a long moment, something unreadable flickering in his eyes. Then, without warning, he straightened and took a step back, his expression still maddeningly calm.

"I don't want to break you," he said, his voice softer now. "But I will if I have to."

Her breath froze at his words, the quiet threat sending a shiver down her spine. But she would not let him see her fear. Not then, and never.

"You can try," she said, her voice steadier than she felt. "But you'll regret it."

A silence stretched between them, thick with tension. Neither of them moved, both too stubborn to back down. It was like a dance, a dangerous, intoxicating dance, where neither wanted to be the first to look away.

She stole a glance at him, her breath catching despite herself. He stood towering over her with broad shoulders, his posture commanding yet somehow effortless.

His chiseled jawline, sharp and strong, was shadowed with the faintest hint of stubble, and his deep-set eyes held an intensity that both unsettled and intrigued her.

He was handsome, too handsome, she thought

bitterly. A man that women would swoon over, even as they hated him for the power he wielded. She hated him for it, too.

Nonetheless, no matter how hard she tried, she couldn't deny the pull he had on her. There was something about the way he looked at her, something primal and raw, that made her pulse quicken.

Her body betrayed her, heating under his gaze, and for the first time in a long time, she felt something she wasn't sure she could control.

She wanted to run and run far away, escape his presence, his power. The truth, however, gnawed at her. She didn't want to leave.

He excited her in ways no man had ever done before, and it terrified her to her core. The thought of surrendering, even for a moment, scared her more than anything she had ever faced.

The day had dragged on, each task more demeaning than the last. By the time evening fell, she was exhausted, her body aching from hours of scrubbing, peeling, and washing.

Her mind was still sharp, still buzzing with the clash of wills she'd had with him.

She couldn't shake the way he looked at her, the way his words had curled around her like a noose. He didn't want to break her, but she wasn't so sure about that.

She'd seen men like him before, men who thought they could control everything and everyone around them. She'd spent her life dodging them, and she planned to do the same.

As she lay on the narrow bed in her small room, staring up at the ceiling and exhausted from the chores, she found herself thinking about him.

She thought about his eyes, the way they had burned into hers with a heat she hadn't expected. She hated him, hated everything he stood for, and being drawn to him was infuriating, and it made her want to scream.

Instead, she closed her eyes and let the exhaustion take over, knowing that tomorrow would bring another battle. Another day of resisting, of fighting against the control he so desperately wanted to have over her.

And as she drifted off to sleep, the thought echoed in her mind: she wouldn't break. No matter what he did, she would never break.

CHAPTER-5

The sky outside the estate was dark with storm clouds, heavy and ominous, as if the weather mirrored the brewing storm inside the house.

She had spent the day in silent rebellion, completing her tasks with deliberate slowness, her every movement filled with defiance.

Each time she passed him, she could feel his eyes on her, watching, judging. It made her skin crawl and her anger simmer just beneath the surface.

She was peeling carrots in the kitchen when the door swung open, and he strode in, his footsteps echoing across the stone floor. She didn't look up, her hands continuing their methodical work, but she could feel the air change, charged with tension.

"I gave you specific instructions." His voice broke through the silence, low and controlled. Too controlled, and she didn't respond.

He stepped closer, his presence looming over her as he spoke again. "You were supposed to finish hours ago."

"And I didn't," she said, her voice flat, barely concealing the anger that burned in her chest. "Guess you'll have to deal with it."

There was a moment of heavy silence, and she could feel his gaze bore into her, pressing down, demanding a response. But she kept her eyes on the task in front of her, refusing to give him the satisfaction of meeting his stare.

Without warning, his hand shot out, grabbing her wrist and stopping her movements. The sharpness of his grip made her flinch, but she refused to show any sign of weakness. Her eyes finally met his, defiant and burning.

"You think you can keep pushing me?" he asked, his voice tight with restrained anger. "You think you can keep testing how far I'll let this go?"

Her pulse quickened, but she wasn't backing down. "I ain't your property. I ain't no one's property." Her voice was a low hiss, filled with venom. "You think just 'cause you're rich, you own everything? Well, you don't own me."

He didn't let go of her wrist, his grip firm but not painful, his eyes locked on hers with an intensity that made her heart race for reasons she didn't want to admit. "You're under my roof," he said slowly, deliberately. "And you're bound by the terms we agreed on."

"Agreed?" she scoffed, yanking her hand free from his grasp. "I didn't agree to nothin'. You forced me into this."

His eyes darkened, and for the first time, she saw the mask of calm he wore slip, revealing the frustration beneath. "You had a choice and could've faced your punishment out there. You'd be dead by now."

"Better dead than trapped here with you," she shot back, her voice shaking with anger. "You think this is any better? I ain't free. I'm still stuck under your thumb."

He stepped closer, his chest barely an inch from hers, and the air between them seemed to thicken with unspoken tension. "Is that what you think?" he asked quietly, his voice laced with something that sent a shiver down her spine. "That I want to control you? To own you?"

She didn't answer, her heart pounding in her chest. The space between them felt too small, too charged, and she hated that her body responded to his presence in ways she couldn't control.

"You're scared," he said, his voice softer now, almost a whisper. "You don't want to admit it, but you're scared of what you feel."

She stepped back, putting distance between them as her breath quickened. "You don't know what you talkin' about," she muttered, but even to her own ears, the words sounded weak, unconvincing.

He didn't move, just stood there, watching her with

those piercing eyes that seemed to see right through her. "I think I do," he whispered. "I think you're fighting because you don't want to feel anything for me. But you do."

She shook her head, trying to force the words out. "I hate you."

"You hate that you don't hate me."

A thick and suffocating silence filled the space as his words hung in the air. She wanted to scream, to throw something, to make him stop talking. Instead, she just stood there, frozen, her heart pounding in her chest as his words sank into her.

He stepped closer again, his voice low and smooth. "You can keep fighting, but sooner or later, you'll have to admit it. This... tension between us. It's not just hate."

She could feel the heat of his body, the closeness of him making it hard to breathe. Her pulse raced, and for a moment, she couldn't tell if it was anger or something else entirely that made her chest tighten.

The space between them seemed to shrink even more, with the undeniable pull that neither of them wanted to name.

"You're wrong," she whispered, her voice shaky but defiant. "I won't give in."

"You already have."

Hours after their confrontation, she lay on the narrow bed in her room, staring up at the ceiling.

The storm outside had finally broken, rain pouring down in heavy sheets, the sound of thunder rumbling in the distance. But the storm inside her was far from over.

She detested him. She had to hate him. There was no other way to make sense of the emotions swirling inside her, the anger, the frustration, the undeniable excitement she felt whenever he was near.

It wasn't just hate, but was something else and it was something dangerous.

She could still feel the heat of his body, the intensity of his gaze. His words echoed in her mind, taunting her, daring her to admit the truth she wasn't ready to face.

He was right, and she hated him for it.

With a frustrated groan, she rolled over, burying her face in the pillow.

She wouldn't give in. She couldn't. No matter how

much her body betrayed her, no matter how much her heart raced when he was near, she wouldn't let him win. She had survived too much to let a man like him break her.

Deep down, she acknowledged that the battle had already been lost, even as the thought crossed her mind. She had already started to plunge down the forbidden well, a treacherous and forbidden action.

The grounds were quiet and drenched in the storm's aftermath. She rose early, before anyone came to fetch her, her body still aching from the day before, her mind a mess of emotions she didn't want to name.

As she made her way downstairs, she was greeted by one of the old maids, another stern woman, who handed her yet a new list of tasks. She didn't care. The routine was almost welcome, something to focus on that wasn't him.

However, as she made her way through the various

rooms of the house, a persistent feeling of being under scrutiny continued to haunt her.

His presence was everywhere, even when he wasn't in the room. And when their paths crossed in the hall, their eyes locked for a moment, the tension still full between them.

Neither of them spoke, but the silence was louder than any argument they could have had. The battle between them wasn't over, not by a long shot.

CHATTER-6

The grand dining room was filled with the glow of the morning sun streaming through the windows.

She tiptoed around the edges of the room, dusting the fine furniture and straightening the already pristine curtains, her mind still turning over the confrontation from before.

She hadn't slept well because every time she closed her eyes, his voice echoed in her mind, his presence lingering in the small space of her room.

The way he had looked at her, the way his words had cut through her defenses, had unnerved her. Made her feel things she didn't want to feel.

He had said she was scared, and damn him, he was right. She wasn't scared of him, though. No, it was something far more dangerous that terrified her.

Footsteps sounded from the hallway, and her heart

leaped in her chest. She didn't need to look up to know who it was. His personality filled the room like a force she couldn't ignore.

She kept her back turned, focusing on the cloth in her hand as she wiped the edge of the table. If she could just keep her focus, pretend he wasn't there…

"You're early today," his voice cut through the quiet, low and smooth. He'd noticed.

She didn't respond, her movements growing more deliberate as she scrubbed the same spot on the table over and over.

"I suppose you're still angry," he continued, stepping closer, his voice taking on a mocking edge. "Last night… it got a little intense, didn't it?"

Her hand paused mid-swipe, her pulse quickening. Of course, he would bring it up. She'd hoped they could pretend it never happened, that she could bury the feelings that had surfaced in that moment of closeness. But he would not let her off that easily.

"I don't know what you're talkin' about," she muttered, turning her back on him and moving to the next piece of furniture.

"Oh, you don't?" He followed her across the room, his presence as inescapable as ever. "So, we're just going to act like nothing happened?"

She stiffened, her grip tightening on the cloth. "Ain't nothin' happened," she said through gritted teeth. "You're makin' things up."

"I don't think I am." His voice was closer now, his

footsteps echoing as he moved toward her. "I think you're scared to admit it."

She whirled around, eyes flashing with anger. "Admit what?" she snapped, her voice louder than she intended. "That you think you can just own me 'cause I'm stuck here working for you? That you think you can say whatever you want and I'm supposed to just... what, fall at your feet?"

His expression darkened, but there was something else in his eyes too that made her heart pound like a drum. "I don't expect you to fall at my feet," he said, his voice quieter now, more serious. "But you can't deny there's something between us."

She opened her mouth to argue, to throw his words back in his face, but the words died on her tongue. Because he was right, and deep down, she knew it.

She had felt the pull between them ever since that first night, and no matter how hard she tried to fight it, it was getting harder to ignore.

She shook her head, taking a step back. "I don't feel nothin' for you."

"Then why are you shaking?" His voice was barely a whisper now, and he took another step toward her, closing the distance between them.

She cursed under her breath, hating how her body betrayed her. Her hands trembled at her sides, and she could feel the heat of him so close, his presence overwhelming her senses.

"You're scared," he repeated, his voice soft but insistent. "You don't want to feel anything for me. But you do."

She shook her head again, her throat tight. "You don't know me."

"I'm starting to," he said, his eyes locked on hers. "And I think you're starting to know me, too."

Her heart was pounding so loud she was sure he could hear it. The way his words got under her skin, making her feel things she didn't want to feel, was something she truly hated.

She wanted to run, to get as far away from him as possible, but her feet wouldn't move and she was rooted to the spot, trapped by the intensity of his gaze.

"I told you," she said, her voice shaking, "I ain't yours."

"No," he whispered, reaching out and gently brushing a strand of hair away from her face. "You're not. But that doesn't mean you don't feel something for me."

The simple touch of his fingers against her skin sent a jolt of electricity through her body. She jerked away, her breath catching in her throat. "Stop it."

He held his hands up in a gesture of surrender, but the look in his eyes told her he wasn't backing down. "I won't push you," he breathed. "But you can't keep lying to yourself."

Later, she sat by the window in her small room, staring out at the sprawling fields beyond the estate.

The sun was setting, and it looked beautiful, but she barely noticed it.

Her mind was still racing, his words from earlier replaying in her head over and over. She hated that he had seen right through her, that he knew exactly what she was feeling even when she didn't want to admit it.

She didn't want to care about him. He was just another rich man, using his power and privilege to control everything around him.

She had been fighting against men like him her entire life, men who thought they could own her, who thought they could break her spirit.

She somehow knew he was different, and that was what scared her the most.

Overwhelmed with frustration, she released a heavy sigh and instinctively hid her face in her hands. She couldn't let this happen, couldn't let herself feel anything for him.

If she did, she would lose everything she had fought so hard to keep, her freedom, her independence, her sense of self.

Was it already too late?

The following morning, she woke with a sense of dread. She knew she couldn't avoid him forever, and part of her didn't even want to, but the fear of what might happen if she let her guard down kept her from seeking him out.

As she worked around the estate, she kept her distance, avoiding him whenever she could. It was only a matter of time before their paths crossed again, even with how gigantic the place was.

It happened in the library, of all places. She had been dusting the shelves when he walked in, his eyes immediately finding her. This time, there was no anger, just an unspoken danger.

He didn't say a word as he moved toward her, his gaze never leaving hers. She stood frozen until he was standing right in front of her, their bodies barely inches apart.

For a long moment, neither of them spoke. The silence was thick, charged with the magnitude of everything they weren't saying. And then, without warning, he reached out and took her hand, his fingers warm and gentle against hers.

She sucked in a sharp breath, her body trembling at the unexpected contact. She wanted to pull away, to keep fighting, but something in his touch stopped her.

"I don't want to fight anymore," he said, his voice barely more than a whisper. "Do you?"

CHAPTER-7

*I*t had been days since their quiet confrontation in the library, but she couldn't stop thinking about it.

The way he had touched her hand so gently, like he was afraid to break her. And the words he had spoken, soft and tentative, had lodged themselves deep in her mind.

"I don't want to fight anymore. Do you?"

His question echoed through her thoughts as she moved through the house, keeping herself busy with her tasks.

She hadn't answered him then. She had only pulled her hand away, her heart racing, and fled from the room like a coward.

She hated she was so confused, so torn between what she wanted and what she knew she shouldn't want. He was her employer, her punishment.

Falling for him would only make things more complicated. Yet, she couldn't deny the hypnotic force that seemed to draw her closer, no matter how hard she tried to resist.

She worked furiously, scrubbing the floor in the hallway, trying to wear herself out.

Maybe if she stayed busy enough, she wouldn't think about him, maybe if she kept moving, she wouldn't feel the ache in her chest every time she remembered his voice, his touch.

Her thoughts were like a relentless pursuer, impossible to outrun. They followed her everywhere, creeping in when she least expected it, and she cursed under her breath, angry at herself for being so weak.

"I can't keep doing this," she muttered, throwing the rag down in frustration. "I ain't some fool to get played."

The sound of footsteps made her freeze. She didn't need to look up to know who it was. His presence was like a shadow that followed her wherever she went, always lurking in the back of her mind.

"You missed a spot," his voice drawled, calm and easy. It seemed to be his favorite thing to say.

She gritted her teeth, refusing to look up. "Maybe if you didn't walk 'round so much, the floor wouldn't need scrubbin'."

He chuckled softly, his boots clicking against the floor as he approached. "I'll take that under consideration."

She could feel his gaze on her, burning into her like the sun on a hot day. Slowly, she lifted her head, meeting his eyes with a defiant glare.

"What do you want?" she snapped, hating how her voice wavered slightly. She wanted to sound strong, unbreakable. His presence always seemed to shake her, no matter how much she tried to steel herself against him.

He tilted his head, studying her for a long moment. "We need to talk."

She snorted, picking up the rag again and turning her back to him. "Ain't nothin' to talk about."

"Oh, I think there is." His voice dropped lower, more serious now. "You've been avoiding me."

"I've been busy, or did you forget how big this place is?"

"Busy running away."

Her shoulders tensed at the accusation, but she didn't turn around. She couldn't face him—not when she knew he was right. She had been running, not just from him, but from herself. From the feelings she didn't want to admit were there.

"I ain't runnin'," she lied, scrubbing the floor harder. "I just got work to do, that's all."

He didn't respond right away, but she could feel him standing there, waiting. The silence between them stretched on, heavy and uncomfortable.

"You can lie to yourself all you want," he said finally,

his voice soft but firm. "But we both know what's happening here."

Her hand stilled on the floor, her heart thudding in her chest. She clenched her jaw, refusing to give in. She would not let him get to her, not again.

"What's happenin'," she said through gritted teeth, "is you think you can control me."

He let out a frustrated sigh, stepping closer. She could feel the heat of him at her back, the space between them growing smaller and smaller. "I don't want to control you as I've said countless times," he said quietly. "I just want you to stop running, stop fighting this."

She stood up abruptly, spinning around to face him. "Fightin' what?" she snapped, her voice louder than she intended. "There ain't nothin' here to fight!"

His eyes darkened, his jaw tightening as he took another step closer. "You really believe that?"

Her breath hiccuped in her throat as he closed the distance between them, his presence overwhelming her senses.

She backed up until she hit the wall, but he didn't stop. He placed a hand on the wall beside her head, trapping her in place.

"Tell me," he said softly, his voice like a caress. "Tell me you don't feel it too."

She opened her mouth to argue, to tell him he was wrong, but the words wouldn't come. It was impossible to lie to him, not when the truth was staring her in the face. She felt it. She felt it every time he was near, every time he looked at her like that, and it scared her.

"I don't..." she whispered, her voice trembling.

"You do," he insisted, his eyes locked on hers. "You feel it just as much as I do."

Her hands clenched into fists at her sides, her body trembling with anger and fear and something else. "It don't matter," she spat, her voice shaking. "You're still just tryin' to own me."

He shook his head, his hand dropping to his side. "I don't want to own you," he whispered. "I want you to be mine."

The vulnerability in his voice caught her off guard, and for a moment, she didn't know how to respond. He wasn't the cold, controlling man she had thought him to be. There was something deeper there, something real. She didn't know if she could trust it, though.

"You don't know what you want," she muttered, turning her head away. "You just think you can have whatever you want 'cause you're rich."

"Maybe I do," he admitted, his voice quiet. "But I know I want you."

Her heart skipped a beat at his words, the raw honesty in his voice sending a shiver down her spine. She had spent her whole life fighting, surviving, never letting anyone get too close. Now, there he was, offering her something she had never thought possible.

However, it came with a price. A price she wasn't sure she was willing to pay.

That night, she lay in her bed in the stark room, staring up at the ceiling. His words echoed in her mind, swirling around her like a storm she couldn't escape.

"I want you."

It was the way he had said it, so quiet, so sure. It seemed like his words went beyond just discussing her physical appearance; there was a deeper meaning behind them.

That it made her heart race was something she strongly disliked. She despised the fact that it stirred up a desire within her to believe him.

She sank onto the bed, the creak of the old frame echoing in the silence of the room. She'd been down this road before, and the memories still stung, like a wound that never quite healed.

Men like him didn't love women like her. She had learned that the hard way, back when she was still stupid enough to believe that kindness could mean something more.

There had been a man years ago, her first actual

glimpse of what she thought was affection. He had promised her the world with soft words and gentle touches, telling her she was special, that he'd take care of her. She had believed him, too.

But when it came time for him to act, when she thought he would lift her out of the life she was living, he revealed his true nature.

He didn't want her for anything more than a passing thrill, and when she refused to give him what he wanted, he turned on her.

His promises became threats, his hands rough and unforgiving. She barely escaped that night, but not without scars. Not without a lesson burned deep into her soul.

That men like him, rich men, powerful men, they didn't care for women like her. They wanted to possess, to take, to use. Love was never part of the bargain.

Why then, why did she feel so torn? Why did the thought of walking away from him make her chest ache?

She let out a frustrated sigh, rolling over onto her side. She needed to clear her head, to stop thinking about him. No matter how hard she tried, she hoped this would be different and maybe this time, she could stop running.

Without giving herself a chance to reconsider, she found herself standing outside his office, hesitating with her hand suspended in mid-air, just inches away from the door.

She didn't know what she was going to say, didn't even know why she was here, but something had pulled her to him and she couldn't ignore it.

Before she could knock, the door swung open, and there he was, standing in front of her with a look of surprise on his face.

"I..." she started, her voice faltering. She had rehearsed this in her head a hundred times, but now that she was standing here, the words wouldn't come.

He stepped aside, opening the door wider. "Come in."

She hesitated for a moment before stepping inside, her heart racing. This was it. This was the moment everything could change.

CHAPTER-8

*S*he sat on the edge of her bed later, staring out the window at the fading light. She'd avoided him all day, slipping in and out of rooms whenever he came near.

The more she tried to run, the more she found herself drawn back to him, like a moth to a flame. And tonight, she knew, something was going to give.

"You always seem to avoid me," he mumbled, his voice soft but laced with frustration. "Why is that?"

She didn't answer, and instead her eyes fixed on the horizon beyond the grounds.

"Talk to me," he urged, stepping further into the room. "I'm not your enemy."

She scoffed, shaking her head. "Ain't you? You got all the power here. I'm just tryin' to survive."

His footsteps drew closer, and then he was standing

right behind her, his warmth seeping into her skin. "Is that all this is to you? Survival?"

She swallowed hard, her throat tight. "Ain't it always?"

There was a long pause before he spoke again, his voice low and serious. "It doesn't have to be."

She finally turned to face him, her eyes burning with a mix of anger and fear. "What else could it be?"

His expression was unreadable, his gaze steady as he looked at her. "It could be something more. If you'd just stop fighting it."

She stood abruptly, putting distance between them. "I ain't fightin' nothin'. You're the one who won't let things be."

He stepped forward, closing the space between them again. "And what if I don't want to let things be?"

Her heart was racing, her breath coming in quick gasps as he loomed over her. She couldn't deny the heat in his eyes or the way her body responded to his nearness.

"What do you want from me?" she demanded, her voice shaking with emotion.

His hand reached up, brushing a strand of hair away from her face. The gesture was so gentle that it made her chest ache. "I want the truth," he murmured, his fingers lingering against her skin. "I want you to admit that you feel it, too."

Her throat tightened, and she pulled away, turning

her back to him again. "I ain't feelin' nothin'," she lied, her voice barely above a whisper.

"Liar," he said softly, his voice filled with both challenge and understanding.

She felt him step closer, his breath warm against the back of her neck. Her entire body tensed, waiting for the inevitable.

She knew what was coming, could feel it in the air between them. Even so, she wasn't prepared for the intensity of it when it finally happened.

Without warning, his hands were on her, pulling her around to face him. Before she could protest, his mouth was on hers, hot and insistent. The kiss was like fire, fierce, burning, and unstoppable. It consumed her, stole the breath from her lungs, and left her dizzy with need.

For a moment, she stood frozen, too shocked to respond. But then something inside her snapped, and all the anger, fear, and desire she had been holding back came flooding out. She kissed him back with equal ferocity, her hands fisting in his shirt as she pressed herself against him.

It was a battle of wills, a clash of power and passion as they fought for control. His hands roamed her body, pulling her closer, while hers pushed against his chest, trying to keep some semblance of distance. But there was no space between them now, no barriers, no walls. Just heat and desire.

His lips moved down to her neck, trailing fire along

her skin as he whispered her name. "You don't have to run anymore," he murmured, his breath hot against her ear. "You don't have to fight."

Her eyes squeezed shut, her breath caught in her throat as she struggled to maintain the control that was slipping through her fingers, just like her resolve. "I can't," she gasped, her hands still pushing against him even as her body betrayed her by leaning into his touch. "I can't trust you."

He pulled back slightly, his dark eyes searching hers. "I'm not asking you to trust me all at once. Just... don't push me away."

She stared up at him, her chest heaving as she tried to catch her breath. Her mind was screaming at her to stop, to run, to protect herself. But her heart? It was saying something else entirely.

She wanted him. As much as she hated to admit it, she wanted him, and that terrified her more than anything.

"I don't know how," she whispered, her voice raw with emotion.

He reached up, cupping her face in his hands. His touch was surprisingly tender, and it made her chest ache in a way she didn't understand. "Then let me show you."

For a long moment, they just stood there, staring at each other. The silence was heavy with unspoken words, unacknowledged feelings. And then, slowly, she nodded.

That night, she didn't sleep. She lay awake, her mind racing with everything that had happened. His touch still lingered on her skin, his words echoing in her ears. "Let me show you."

Could she really let her guard down? Could she really trust him, after everything she had been through?

Her heart was still pounding, her body still humming with the memory of his kiss and the way his hands had cupped her breasts through her simple dress. She had never felt anything like it before, so raw, so powerful. It scared her, but it also made her want more. She'd wanted him to rip it off her body and truly claim her, but he'd controlled himself, like a true gentleman.

"Only when you're fully ready," he'd said as he let her go and she'd fled on rubbery legs.

There was still a gulf of difference between them, race, class, upbringing. The list went on and on, and she didn't know if they could ever truly bridge that gap.

She sat up, wrapping her arms around her knees as she stared out the window. The night was quiet, the stars twinkling in the sky. Everything seemed so peaceful, so still. Inside, she was a whirlwind of emotions, conflicted, confused, and completely overwhelmed.

The next day, things were different. She could feel it in the air, in the way he looked at her when she entered the room. The tension between them had changed to something more complicated.

They didn't talk about the kiss, didn't mention the way they had both lost control. However, it was undeniably there, suspended in the air, causing a heavy burden that neither of them could disregard.

He watched her as she went about her tasks, his eyes following her every movement. She could feel the heat of his gaze, the unspoken desire simmering just below the surface. When every time their eyes met, her heart skipped a beat.

She wasn't ready to talk about it. Not yet. She needed time to process, to figure out what it all meant.

So she kept her distance, kept her head down, and tried to pretend like nothing had changed. In her innermost thoughts, she knew everything had.

CHAPTER-9

*T*he next few days passed in a blur of awkward silences and stolen glances. The kiss had changed something between them, and no matter how hard she tried to pretend otherwise, she couldn't deny it.

He was watching her, always watching her. His eyes followed her like a shadow, dark and intense, burning with something she didn't want to name. Every time their eyes met, her heart skipped a beat, and she held her breath, waiting for something to happen, but nothing did. He didn't touch her again. He didn't even try, and in a way, that made it worse.

The distance between them felt like a chasm, growing wider with every passing day. She knew he was waiting for her to make the first move, to acknowledge what had happened between them. But she wasn't ready, not yet.

Instead, she threw herself into her work, scrubbing floors and washing linens with a ferocity that left her hands raw and her body aching. She needed the distraction, needed something to occupy her mind so she wouldn't have to think about him. He was always there, though, lurking in the back of her mind.

And at night, when the house was quiet, and the world was still, she lay awake in her bed, staring at the ceiling and remembering the way his lips had felt on hers. The way his hands had gripped her, possessive and gentle all at once. The way he had looked at her, like she was the only thing in the world that mattered.

She hated herself for wanting more.

It was late in the afternoon when she finally couldn't take it anymore. She was in the kitchen, her hands deep in soapy water as she scrubbed the dishes from lunch, when she felt him behind her. She didn't turn around, didn't acknowledge his presence, even as her nipples stiffened.

"Are you just gonna keep avoiding me forever?" His voice was low, but there was an edge to it that made her heart race.

She didn't answer, her hands moving faster as she scrubbed the plate in front of her. Maybe if she just kept working, kept her head down, he would leave her alone.

But he didn't.

"Talk to me," he said, stepping closer. "I will not let you run from this."

She finally stopped, her hands stilling in the water as she took a deep breath. "Ain't nothin' to talk about."

"Don't lie to me." His tone was sharp, demanding.

She spun around, her eyes blazing with defiance. "What would you like me to say? That I felt something and have been thinking about it ever since? That I hate myself for wantin' more?

The words were out before she could stop them, and the second they left her mouth, she regretted them. Her heart was pounding, her chest tight as she waited for his response.

But instead of anger, his expression softened, his eyes lit with relief. "And why do you hate yourself for wanting more?" he asked quietly.

"Because I ain't supposed to want it," she whispered, her voice trembling. "You and me...we ain't supposed to..."

"Who says we ain't?" he interrupted, stepping closer. His voice was calm, but there was a fierceness in his eyes that made her pulse quicken. "You've been fighting this since the day we met. Why?"

"Because I can't trust you!" she blurted, her emotions spilling out in a rush. "You got all the power here. You can do whatever you want, and I ain't got no say in it. I can't let myself…"

Her voice broke, and she turned away, blinking back the tears that threatened to spill over. She hated feeling weak, hated letting him see just how vulnerable she was.

Rather than retreating, he stood his ground and did not back down. Instead, he reached out, gently turning her to face him again. "I don't expect you to trust me all at once," he said softly. "But you gotta stop pushing me away."

She swallowed hard, her throat tight. "I've told you I don't know how."

"Let go, and you will."

His words were so simple, so sincere, that for a moment, she almost believed him. But the fear was still there, skulking beneath the surface, whispering to her that this was dangerous. That letting him in could destroy her.

"I ain't ready," she said, her voice barely above a whisper.

"I'm not going anywhere," he promised, his hand still resting lightly on her arm. "When you're ready, I'll be here."

That night, as she lay in bed, she couldn't stop

thinking about his words. The way he had looked at her, the way he had touched her. It had felt different this time, not like before, when it was all heat and passion. This time was different, but just as powerful.

She wasn't sure if she was ready for that; she wasn't sure if she could handle it.

She had spent her whole life surviving, doing whatever it took to get by. Letting someone in, trusting someone, that was dangerous. And trusting someone like him, with all his power and privilege? That was terrifying.

But the small, stubborn part of her wanted to believe him. Wanted to believe that maybe he was different.

The next morning, when she went downstairs to start her chores, he was waiting for her. She froze in the doorway, her heart thumping as their eyes met.

"Good morning," he said, his voice calm, almost casual. But there was a glint in his eyes that told her he hadn't forgotten their conversation.

"Mornin'," she mumbled, keeping her head down as she walked past him.

But as she moved toward the kitchen, he stopped her, his hand gently catching her arm. "Wait."

She paused, her heart sprinting as she looked up at him.

"I meant what I said last night," he whispered, his eyes searching hers. "I am not going to push you, but I need you to know that I'm not just gonna give up, either."

Her throat tightened, and for a moment, she didn't know what to say. Part of her wanted to push him away again, to run from the feelings that scared her so much. But another part of her, that betraying part she had been trying to ignore, wanted to stay. Wanted to see where this could go.

She swallowed hard, her voice barely above a whisper. "I still don't know if I can trust you."

"I know you've had a rough life," he said, his voice soft but steady. "But maybe you can start by not running from me."

CHAPTER-10

*T*he days that followed weren't easy. She had taken his words to heart, about not running, about staying, but it was harder than she had imagined.

Every time she let her guard down, even for a second, the fear crept back in. Fear that she was letting herself be vulnerable.

Fear that he could break her heart just as easily as he had kissed her. The more time she spent with him, however, the more she saw a different side of him, one she hadn't expected or hadn't wanted to see.

She had initially thought he was much crueler than he actually was. He wasn't like the others, the men who looked at her like she was nothing more than a piece of property, a tool to be used and discarded.

He watched her differently too, his gaze filled with something more than just desire. And when he spoke to her, there was a softness in his tone that made her heart ache.

She didn't know what to do with that.

The next morning, she woke early, with the house was still, the air cool with the promise of a new day. Slipping out of bed, she dressed quickly and made her way downstairs, ready to start her chores.

When she entered the kitchen, she was surprised to find him already there, sitting at the table with a cup of coffee in hand.

He looked up when she entered, his eyes meeting hers. For a moment, neither of them spoke. Then he nodded toward the stove. "Made some coffee. Figured you could use a cup."

She hesitated, her eyes narrowing with suspicion. "What's your game?"

He raised an eyebrow, taking a sip from his mug. "There's no game. Just thought you might want some before you get started."

Her eyes flicked to the steaming pot on the stove, then back to him. It was strange, this casual offer of kindness. She wasn't used to it and it made her more uneasy than if he'd been trying to corner her.

"I can make my own," she muttered, moving past him to grab a cup.

He didn't stop her, but she could feel his eyes on her as she poured herself a mug. She sipped the coffee; the warmth soothing her nerves. The unsaid words seemed to speak volumes.

"You don't have to keep fighting me, you know," he sighed after a moment, his voice calm but firm. "No one here is gonna hurt you."

Her grip tightened around the cup. "Maybe not you, but I still don't trust nobody in this house."

He leaned back in his chair, his gaze steady. "I get that. Trust doesn't come all at once. It's earned, little by little."

She didn't respond, but his words stuck with her as she went about her chores. Was he really trying to earn her trust? And if he was, did she want to give it to him?

The quiet of the morning didn't last. By noon, the house was alive with activity as guests arrived, men in fine clothes and women in elaborate dresses, all laughing and chattering as they filled the parlor.

As a lowly staff member, there had been no reason for her to be informed, she thought scornfully.

She stayed out of the way, keeping to the kitchen and the back hallways where no one would notice her. However, she could hear them, their voices drifting through the open doors.

Every so often, she caught a glimpse of him in the crowd, his posture stiff as he played the part of the gracious host.

She wasn't sure what bothered her more, the way he seemed so comfortable in that world or the way it reminded her she didn't belong in it.

By late afternoon, the guests were gathered outside, the men smoking cigars and discussing business while the women sat in the shade, fanning themselves. She was in the garden, trimming the hedges, when she overheard two men talking.

"Your new maid's got some fire in her," one of them said with a chuckle. "I saw the way she looked at you. Reckon she's just waiting for a chance to sink her claws in."

She froze, her heart pounding as she realized they were talking about her. She couldn't see their faces from where she stood, but she knew their type: men who thought women like her were nothing more than prey.

His voice came next, calm but with an edge of steel. "Watch your tongue. You don't get to talk about her."

There was a brief silence, and then the other man laughed. "Didn't mean any harm. Just saying is all. There's no point getting too attached to them though because they come and go, you know that."

Her breath caught in her throat, her hands trembling as she waited for his response.

"She's different," he said, his voice quiet but firm. "And you'd do well to remember that."

Her heart clenched at his words. Part of her wanted to run, to get as far away from him and his world as she could. The other part she didn't fully understand wanted to believe him. Wanted to believe that she was different to him.

Later that evening, after the guests had left, she found him alone in his study. She wasn't sure what had driven her there. Maybe it was the way he had defended her, or maybe it was the way his words had made her feel something she wasn't ready to admit.

He looked up as she entered, his expression unreadable. "What is it?"

She stood in the doorway, her arms crossed tightly over her chest. "Why'd you say that?"

His brow furrowed. "Say what?"

"That I'm different." Her voice was sharper than she intended, but she couldn't help it. "Why'd you say that to him?"

He leaned back in his chair, his eyes darkening as they met hers. "Because you are."

Her heart pounded in her chest. "I ain't no different from anyone else. I'm just…"

"Just what?" he interrupted, his voice low but intense. "You think I don't see who you are? You think I don't know what you're capable of?"

She shook her head, her throat tight. "I don't know what you want from me."

"I want nothing from you except the truth." He stood, closing the distance between them in a few quick strides. "You've been running since the day I brought you here, but you can't run forever."

Her pulse quickened as he reached out, gently cupping her chin in his hand. His touch was warm, his eyes searching hers.

"You're not like the others," he said quietly. "I see you and I will not let you pretend you don't matter."

Her walls crumbled in that moment, and she felt tears prick at the corners of her eyes. She had spent so long pretending to be strong, pretending that nothing could touch her. The truth was that she had never felt so vulnerable.

"You don't know me, what I've done in the past," she whispered, her voice trembling.

"Maybe not all of you," he admitted, his thumb brushing her cheek. "But I want to."

CHAPTER-11

*S*he didn't know how long she had stood
there, staring at the closed door after their
confrontation the night before.

Her mind had replayed his words repeatedly: *"I see
you."* It was too much, too close. And yet, she hadn't
been able to deny the warmth that crept into her chest
when he said it.

That day, as she went about her duties, the feeling
of unease lingered. She wasn't sure what had changed,
but something between them had shifted, and she
didn't know if that was a good thing.

He had been watching her again. Not the way he
used to, like she was some wild animal he needed to
tame. No, now there, in his gaze, was something that
made her heart race and her stomach twist in knots.

She didn't like it. At least, that's what she kept
telling herself.

That afternoon, she was hanging sheets on the line behind the house when one of the men who worked the stables approached her. His name was Earl, and he had always been too bold for her liking, his eyes lingering on her longer than necessary.

"Well, ain't you lookin' pretty today," Earl said, his voice thick with a leering smile. He stepped closer, invading her space, and she instinctively took a step back.

"Don't you got work to do?" she snapped, her voice sharper than usual. She didn't have time for his nonsense today.

Earl chuckled, taking another step closer. "Don't be like that now. Just tryin' to be friendly."

Her hands clenched into fists at her sides, her heart pounding in her chest. She wasn't afraid of him, not exactly, but she knew men like Earl. She knew what they were capable of.

Before she could respond, she heard a voice from behind her.

"Step away from her."

She turned to see him standing on the porch, his eyes dark and dangerous as he stared down at Earl. For a moment, she thought the idiot might try to stand his ground. He knew better, though. You don't mess with the hands that feed you.

The once smug expression on his face faded, and he stepped back in response. "Didn't mean no harm," he muttered before turning and walking away, glancing back only once.

She finally allowed herself to sigh after she'd seen the back of him.

"Are you all right?" His voice was softer now, concerned.

She didn't answer right away. Instead, she turned her back on him and continued hanging over the sheets, her hands trembling slightly.

"I didn't need your help," she muttered, her voice barely audible.

He was silent for a moment, and she wondered if he would just leave her there, let her stew in her own stubbornness.

She felt him behind her, close enough that she could feel the heat of his body, though he didn't touch her.

"You shouldn't have to defend yourself against men like him," he said quietly.

She spun around to face him, her eyes blazing with anger. "Men like him? What about men like you? You think I forgot where I am? That I forgot who you are?"

He didn't flinch at her words. Instead, he held her gaze, his expression unreadable.

"I am nothing like him," he said, his voice low and steady. "And you know it."

She hated the way his words made her feel, the way they chipped away at her defenses. She wanted to fight him, to push him away, but the truth was, she didn't have the strength.

"Why do you care so much, huh?" she demanded, her voice shaking. "Why are you doing this?"

His eyes softened, and for a moment, she saw something in them that scared her more than anything else: vulnerability.

"I don't know," he admitted, his voice barely above a whisper. "But I do."

She felt her resolve crumbling again, her anger slipping through her fingers like sand. She wanted to hold on to it, to keep that wall between them, but it was getting harder every day.

"I don't need nobody to protect me," she muttered, turning away from him.

"I know," he said softly. "But that doesn't mean I won't."

That evening, she found herself outside on the porch, staring up at the stars. The night was cool, and the air smelled of pine and earth, a familiar scent that had always brought her comfort. That night, it felt different, like the world was shifting beneath her feet, and she didn't know how to stand still.

She heard the door creak behind her and figured it was him. The house had been still when she left her room and she figured everyone was asleep. He said nothing at first, just stood beside her, staring out into the dark.

After a long silence, he spoke. "You ever wonder what it'd be like to just... leave? Get away from all this?"

He knew the thought had crossed her mind many times.

She glanced at him, surprised by the question. "Where would I go?" she asked, her voice tinged with bitterness. "Ain't nowhere in this world for someone like me."

His jaw tightened, and he looked away, his hands clenched into fists at his sides. "You're wrong," he said quietly. "There's always somewhere. Just depends on whether you're brave enough to find it. I think by your choosing to stay here means that you're brave enough."

She blinked hard because she knew he was telling the truth. Every time she thought about leaving that place, she changed her mind quickly. She liked not having to lie and steal to survive; she enjoyed having food, and she even liked the routine. More than that, she knew she stayed because of him. Everything else was just a bonus. He had gotten under her skin.

She frowned, pretending not to understand what he was getting at. But before she said anything, he turned and walked back into the house, leaving her alone with her thoughts.

CHAPTER-12

*S*he awoke with a start, disturbed by her dreams. It was always the same. The kiss that had been more than just a kiss. It had been a breaking point, a crossing of a line she swore she'd never approach.

Her lips still tingled from the memory, but then the same lips tightened with regret.

She swung her legs over the edge of the bed, her hands trembling as she pulled on her work clothes. She felt different today, like something had shifted inside her and she wasn't ready to face it.

Outside her door, the house was silent. Too silent. She had grown used to the soft hum of activity, the distant voices of the staff. But that morning, everything was still as if waiting for an event to happen.

The moment she walked into the kitchen, she could feel the heavy atmosphere of tension surrounding her.

Her presence caused the other women's eyes to flicker briefly before looking away. The silence wasn't just her imagination. They had noticed something. *They knew.* That nasty man, Earl, must have spread rumors.

Her chest tightened because it was the very thing she had been trying to avoid, being noticed, becoming a part of something more than survival. She needed to get out, needed to run. But where would she go?

Later that morning, while she was cleaning in the parlor, he entered, but she glanced away as soon as their eyes met, and focused on her work.

He cleared his throat, his voice unnaturally formal. "Good morning."

She stiffened, not sure what to say. "Mornin'."

The silence that followed was unbearable. He stood awkwardly by the door, as if unsure whether to come closer or leave. His presence filled the room, suffocating her with its weight.

Finally, he broke the silence. "About last night—"

"Don't," she interrupted, her voice sharp and defensive. "Don't say nothin' about it."

He stared at her, his expression a mixture of confusion and frustration. "We need to talk about it."

She spun around to face him, her eyes blazing. "Talk about what? It was a mistake. That's all it was."

His jaw clenched, the muscles in his neck tightening as he fought to stay calm. "A mistake? Is that really what you think?"

She forced herself to hold his gaze, even though the

intensity of it made her knees weak. "I ain't got time for no foolishness," she muttered. "I got work to do."

Without another word, she turned her back on him and continued cleaning, her hands shaking as she scrubbed the surface of the table.

But she could feel his eyes on her, burning into her back. And deep down, she knew he would not let this go.

The tension between them only grew as the days passed. He never brought up the conversation or their kiss again, but whenever they were together, it was a perpetual reminder.

She hated the way he made her feel, so out of control, so vulnerable. She hated herself more for wanting him, for needing him in ways that scared her.

One afternoon, the silence between them finally broke.

"Why are you doing this?" he asked, his voice filled with frustration.

She glanced at him, confused. "Doin' what?"

He stepped closer, his eyes intense. "Pushing me away. Pretending like what happened between us meant nothing."

She crossed her arms over her chest, trying to shield herself from his words. "'Cause it didn't," she lied. "It don't mean nothin'."

He let out a bitter laugh. "You're a terrible liar."

She scowled, turning her back on him. "Ain't

nothin' to talk about. You got your life, I got mine. We ain't the same."

"But we could be," he said quietly, his voice softening.

She froze, her heart pounding in her chest. *Could be? What did he mean by that?*

"Why do you care so much?" she muttered, her voice barely audible. It was impossible for a man like him to like a woman like her.

"I don't know," he admitted, his voice filled with raw emotion. "But I do. And I can't stop."

His words pierced through her defenses, shaking her to the core. She wanted to run, to escape the intensity of his gaze, but her feet refused to move.

She whirled around to face him, her chest heaving with emotion. "You don't know nothin' about me," she spat, her voice trembling. "You don't know what it's like. Every day is a fight just to survive."

"I know more than you think," he said quietly.

She shook her head, tears burning in her eyes. "You got everything. You ain't never had to beg, never had to steal just to get by."

He stepped closer, closing the distance between them. "And I'd give it all up, every bit, if it meant keeping you safe."

Her breath caught in her throat at his words. She stared at him, her mind racing. Why was he saying this? Why was he willing to risk everything for her?

"Why?" she whispered, her voice barely audible.

He reached out and gently cupped her face, his thumb brushing away a tear that had slipped down her cheek. "Because I see you," he murmured. "The real you. And I can't walk away from that."

His words broke something inside her, shattering the last of her defenses. She felt the weight of all her fears and insecurities crashing down on her, overwhelming her.

Without thinking, she reached out and grabbed the front of his shirt, pulling him closer. "Don't," she whispered, her voice filled with desperation. "Don't make me need you."

His arms wrapped around her, pulling her into his chest. "It's too late," he whispered against her hair. "I already do."

CHAPTER-13

$\mathcal{T}$he tension between them hung in the air after the events of the previous night.

She had expected things to remain the same, her place as his maid, a temporary arrangement for her to work off her "punishment," but when he called her into his study that morning, she sensed something had shifted.

She entered the room cautiously, her eyes sweeping over the luxurious furniture, the tall shelves filled with books she couldn't read, and he, standing behind the desk, arms crossed, watching her.

"I've made a decision," he began, his voice low and commanding, yet gentle. "I've seen potential in you, something far beyond what you believe in yourself."

Her heart pounded, and she raised her chin slightly, always defiant. "And what's that supposed to mean?"

He stepped closer, his gaze softening as he studied

her. "You've survived in ways that show you're stronger than most. But survival isn't all there is. I want you to thrive."

She furrowed her brow, confusion mingling with suspicion. "Thrive? I'm just a maid."

"You won't be a maid much longer," he said, his voice firm. "I've arranged for a teacher, someone to help you learn, etiquette, language, the things you need to become more... refined."

Her stomach churned at the thought. *A teacher?* What did he expect her to be? A proper lady? "You think you can turn me into one of your fancy society women?" she asked, her voice laced with sarcasm. "Someone who sits pretty and says all the right things? You must be as cray as a loon."

His jaw tightened, but he didn't waver. "You'll never be like them. And I don't want you to be. I want you to become the best version of yourself."

She stared at him, trying to make sense of his words. *Why would he want that?* No one had ever wanted more for her than what she already had, a life of scraping by.

"You have a choice," he added, sensing her reluctance. "You can stay the way you are, or you can learn, grow, and take control of your own future."

Her throat tightened as she tried to suppress the emotions welling up inside her. She had always been in control of her own fate, or so she thought. But now, faced with the prospect of becoming someone different, someone better, she wasn't sure if she was ready.

The next day, the teacher arrived. Miss Lillian Worthington, an elegant woman in her mid-thirties, stepped into the grand foyer. Her presence was striking, poised and refined, with an air of authority that made even the maids stand a little straighter.

She approached the woman with a warm, practiced smile, but there was an undercurrent of seriousness in her eyes. "You must be the student, Zelena," she said, extending her hand. "I'm Miss Everwood. I'll be guiding you through this journey."

Zelena hesitated, her instincts screaming at her to run, to resist the very idea of being "guided" by anyone. Something about Miss Everwood's confidence drew her in. She shook her hand reluctantly.

"I don't need no fancy lessons," she muttered, crossing her arms defensively. "I'm fine the way I am."

Miss Everwood didn't flinch. "Everyone is fine the

way they are," she replied calmly. "But we can always become more."

With that, the lessons began. Miss Everwood wasted no time diving into the world of etiquette, how to sit properly, how to walk with grace, how to hold herself with dignity. Zelena struggled with every step, her movements awkward, her speech rough, her patience thin.

She gritted her teeth through every correction, her body stiff as she tried to mimic the elegance of the teacher. She felt lots of eyes on her and heard giggles because she was being watched by the other maids who delighted in her misfortune.

"Hold your back straight," Miss Everwood instructed, her voice calm but firm. "A lady never slouches. Posture is everything."

She rolled her eyes, but complied, feeling foolish. "Why does it even matter how I sit?"

"It matters because it shows control," Miss Everwood explained, her gaze steady. "A lady controls how the world perceives her."

The woman's defiance flared. "I don't care how the world sees me. They ain't never cared about me before."

Miss Everwood paused, her expression softening. "You should care," she said gently. "Because once you control how others see you, you'll realize you have a lot of power you didn't know you had."

Later that night, after hours of frustrating lessons, she sat by the fireplace in the enormous kitchen, which was empty save for her, her hands curled into fists.

She had hated every minute, the forced elegance, the way she had to hold herself, the constant corrections. It all felt unnatural, like she was trying to be something she wasn't.

He entered the room quietly, watching her from the doorway for a moment before speaking. "How did it go?"

She shot him a glare. "How do you think? I ain't cut out for this. I ain't never gonna be a lady."

He walked over to her, crouching down so they were at eye level. "It's not about being a 'lady.' It's about showing the world what you're capable of."

She shook her head, the frustration boiling over. "I'm capable of surviving. I don't need to be no pretty little thing in a dress."

He reached out, gently placing a hand on hers. "This

isn't about making you something you're not. It's about giving you the tools to be whoever you want to be."

His words struck a chord deep within her, stirring something she had tried to bury. She had spent so long fighting, surviving, that she had never stopped to think about what she *could* be.

But it scared her. The idea of letting go of the person she had always been, the raw, untamed woman who had fought for every scrap of life.

"I don't know if I can do it," she whispered, her voice shaking.

"You can," he said firmly, his eyes never leaving hers. "You're stronger than you think."

The next morning, she stood in front of the mirror in one room downstairs, staring at her reflection. Miss Everwood had dressed her in a simple, yet elegant gown. It wasn't as extravagant as the dresses the society women wore, but it was a far cry from the rags she had been used to.

Her hair was neatly pulled back, and though she felt out of place in the clothes, she couldn't deny that she looked... different. More refined. More controlled.

She hated how much she liked it.

Miss Everwood entered the room, observing her silently for a moment before speaking. "You look beautiful."

She scoffed, though there was no real venom behind it. "I look ridiculous."

"Not at all," Miss Everwood replied. "You look like a woman who is realizing her worth."

She didn't respond, her eyes still locked on the reflection in the mirror. The woman staring back at her was both familiar and foreign, a version of herself she had never imagined.

The thought occurred to her that maybe she could become that woman after all.

The atmosphere in the household had shifted, and everyone knew why. The servants spoke in hushed whispers, casting glances her way, aware that something had changed.

It was no secret that the master had taken a fancy to her, and while some of the staff were filled with envy, others looked at her with something close to admiration.

To be in her position, elevated from a maid to something more, even if no one dared say it aloud, was a rare, enviable fate. Zelena's room had been moved too, now in a more spacious, sunlit corner of the house, far from the cramped quarters where the other maids slept.

She no longer scrubbed floors or washed linens; her days were now devoted entirely to learning, to reading, writing, etiquette, and language, shaping her into something more refined.

It was a strange feeling, not working, but being groomed for something else entirely. As she walked the grounds, she noticed that Earl, the big-mouthed henchman who always had a lewd comment to share, had disappeared.

No one spoke of him, and though she never found out what became of him, she had a feeling she knew. The master made sure things were handled quietly when it suited him.

CHAPTER-14

$\mathcal{D}$ays turned into weeks, and the lessons with Miss Everwood became a constant in her life. Each morning, she was up at dawn, practicing everything from how to pour tea to how to respond to an invitation with elegance.

The progress was slow, frustrating, and filled with moments where she nearly gave up entirely.

The rich man, *her* man, as she had started to think of him in quiet, stolen moments, watched from a distance, giving her space to adjust.

Every time she felt ready to walk away, to return to her old self, his steady presence kept her grounded.

One afternoon, Miss Everwood was teaching her how to curtsy. Her knees wobbled as she lowered herself, trying to mimic the grace of a woman who had known this world her whole life.

"No, no," Miss Everwood corrected softly, guiding

her shoulders back into place. "It's all about balance. Don't fight your body, trust it."

"I'm trying," she muttered, frustrated. "But it ain't natural. I mean, it's not natural," she corrected herself.

Miss Everwood smiled faintly. "It doesn't have to feel natural. It just has to feel like you. You're not becoming someone else, but refining who you already are."

She sighed, straightening up again and shaking out her arms. "I don't know if I'll ever get it."

"You will," Miss Everwood reassured her, stepping back. "But you need to stop thinking of it as changing who you are. Think of it as adding more tools to your arsenal. You've survived all this time. Imagine what you can do when the world doesn't see you as a survivor, but as a force."

Those words sat with her long after the lesson ended.

That evening, after yet another exhaustive day, she

stood at the large windows overlooking the garden, watching the sunset.

The sky was a swirl of colors, orange, pink, purple, but she barely noticed it. Her mind was a storm of thoughts, doubts, and feelings unexplainable.

He came to stand beside her, silent at first, just watching her as he often did. She could feel his gaze on her like it always did. After what felt like an eternity, he finally spoke.

"How are the lessons going?"

She didn't turn to look at him. "It's hard. Feels like I'm trying to be something I'm not."

His brow furrowed. "What do you mean?"

She clenched her fists, her frustration bubbling up. "All this—" she gestured vaguely to the elegant dress she wore, the neat hair, the perfectly polished nails. "It's not me. I don't know how to be this."

He stepped closer, his voice soft but firm. "I don't want you to be anyone other than who you are."

"Then why are you doing this?" she snapped, turning to face him. Her eyes flashed with the fire that had kept her alive for so long. "Why are you trying to turn me into some lady when I ain't ever gonna be one?"

He took her by the shoulders, his grip gentle but steady. "Because I believe in you. I believe you can be anything you want to be. You're more than what you think of yourself."

Her breath caught in her throat. No one had ever

believed in her before. No one had ever told her she could be *more*.

"You don't have to change," he continued, his voice low and intense. "But if you want to, if you want to be more, I'll help you. I'll give you everything you need to succeed. But you have to want it."

Her heart pounded in her chest, the raw intensity of his words crashing into her. She had never been offered something like this before. Some freedom, yes, but not opportunity. Not the chance to rise above the life she had always known.

Tears welled up in her eyes, and she tried to blink them away. She didn't want to be vulnerable, not in front of him. But the walls she had built around herself were crumbling under his gaze.

"Sometimes I wonder if you're just wasting your time because I don't know if I can do it," she whispered, her voice trembling.

"You can," he said, brushing a strand of hair away from her face. "I know you can."

The next day, something changed in her. She woke up with a renewed sense of determination, though the fear still lingered in the back of her mind.

She wasn't sure she was ready to become the woman he saw in her, but she was willing to try.

Miss Everwood noticed the shift immediately.

"You're standing taller today," she remarked as they began their lesson. "Something on your mind?"

She shrugged, a faint smile tugging at the corner of her lips. "I guess I just realized... maybe I can do this."

Miss Everwood smiled, her eyes twinkling with approval. "That's the first step. Believing in yourself."

The lesson that day was about conversation, how to speak with confidence, and how to engage with others in polite society. It was something she struggled with, having spent most of her life avoiding attention rather than commanding it.

"Remember," Miss Everwood instructed, "you are not lesser than anyone you speak to. You have the right to be heard."

She repeated the words in her mind, trying to internalize them. *I have the right to be heard. That was a hard thing to realize when one was born into slavery. Society made sure that her right to be heard was wiped out.*

The words felt foreign to her tongue, but the more she said them, the more she started to believe them.

Her transformation wasn't just about learning how to dress or speak like a lady, but it was about discovering a new power.

For so long, she had relied on her instincts to survive, on her ability to blend into the shadows and go unnoticed. But now, she was learning how to stand out, how to take control of a room with her presence.

She tested her newfound confidence one evening during dinner. The servants had set the table with fine china, and the candlelight flickered softly against the crystal glasses.

He sat at the head of the table, watching her as she carefully cut into her meal, every movement deliberate and measured.

It wasn't just the way she handled herself, but the way she spoke. When he asked her a question, she didn't mumble her response or avert her eyes. She looked him directly in the eye and spoke with clarity, her voice steady and strong.

"You're learning fast," he remarked, a hint of admiration in his voice.

She smirked, feeling a surge of pride. "I guess I have an excellent teacher."

His eyes darkened slightly as he regarded her, and she felt the tension between them shift to something more intense. There was a new dynamic between them now.

He wasn't just the man who had saved her from the streets; he was the one guiding her transformation. In the process, however, she was changing him, too.

As the meal continued, she laughed, the sound surprising to herself. It was a small thing, but it marked a turning point. She wasn't just surviving anymore; she was starting to live.

CHAPTER-15

*D*ays passed, and with every lesson, every conversation, she felt the old version of herself slipping away. Not that she was losing who she was, but she was developing, refining.

Miss Everwood was relentless, but kind, correcting her posture, speech, and movements with a sharp eye for detail.

But it was him, *the man* who lingered in her mind. Each evening, they shared meals, conversations, and fleeting glances that held more than mere curiosity.

The tension between them thickened like a storm waiting to break, and she could feel it every time his eyes followed her across the room. Unlike what another man would have done, he did not force himself on her, and she felt grateful for his restraint.

One particular evening, the air was filled with the

scent of gardenia, and the house was alive with the faint sounds of a distant ball in town.

He stood near the fireplace, sipping a glass of brandy, while she carefully placed the last silver spoon on the dining table. Her movements had become more graceful, deliberate, though there was still a rawness beneath the surface.

"You look more confident," he said, his voice breaking the silence.

She glanced up at him, her eyes meeting his. "Maybe I'm just tired of being afraid."

He smiled faintly, nodding as though understanding something unspoken. "Fear doesn't suit you."

They shared a moment of silence, and as his words sank in, she could feel them drape over her like a heavy cloak. For so long, her life had been defined by fear.

The fear of being caught, fear of never being good enough, fear of losing her life. But now, in this house, under his watchful gaze, that fear was fading.

"I wasn't always afraid," she admitted softly, her hands smoothing out the edge of the tablecloth. "Before all this, I had dreams, things I wanted for myself."

He set his glass down, crossing the room to stand beside her. His presence was overwhelming, but she didn't shrink away. Instead, she looked up at him, meeting his gaze with a steady, defiant stare.

"What did you want?" he asked, his voice an inaudible murmur.

She hesitated, the words catching in her throat. She

wasn't used to sharing her dreams, especially not with someone like him. However, there was something in the way he gazed at her that evoked a certain emotion within her. Safety.

"I wanted to be more than what I was born into," she finally said. "I wanted to have choices."

He studied her for a long moment, his expression unreadable. Then, without warning, he reached out and gently touched her chin, lifting her face toward his.

His warm breath gently caressed her skin as he whispered, reminding her she was much more than she realized. "You've always had choices, but just didn't know it yet."

Her heart pounded in her chest, but, instead of leaning in, instead of crossing that final line, he dropped his hand and took a step back.

Ever the gentleman, but she was tiring of that.

***

The next morning, she awoke to a knock on her

door. Miss Everwood entered with a glint in her eye, carrying a dress of deep emerald silk.

"What's this for?" she asked, eyeing the gown suspiciously.

"You're invited to a ball tonight," Miss Everwood explained, hanging the dress on the wardrobe. "It's time to put what you've learned into practice."

Her stomach twisted into knots. A ball? She hadn't expected to be thrust into society so soon, especially not into a world that would surely judge her for everything she wasn't.

"I don't belong there," she muttered, staring at the dress as though it were a weapon meant to destroy her.

Miss Everwood smiled. "That's where you're wrong. You belong wherever you decide to be. And tonight, you're going to show them that."

Of course, Lucien must have thought she was ready.

Lucien, a name she had refused to use at first, clinging to the scornful titles she'd called him in the beginning, "the master," "her jailer," and other names filled with venom.

He had insisted, with that commanding tone of his, that she stop calling him those horrid names and call him by his real one. At first, it had felt strange on her tongue, like wearing shoes that didn't quite fit.

Over time, though, she'd grown used to it, and now, every time she said "Lucien," a strange warmth would creep into her voice that she didn't quite understand.

Sometimes, when she was alone in her room, she'd daydream and let his name roll softly off her tongue, her lips curling into a secret smile. It was alarming how his name alone stirred her dreams.

~ ~ ~

The moment Zelena's fingers brushed the fabric of the gown, she felt a strange flutter in her chest. It was softer than anything she had ever worn before, the silk cool against her skin as the maids helped her step into it.

They fussed over the fit, tying the ribbons in place, adjusting the bodice, and smoothing every inch of the dress with precision.

For the first time, she wasn't in the plain clothes of a maid, but in something meant to transform her. And yet, as she looked at herself in the mirror, there was a part of her that couldn't help but feel like an imposter.

"This isn't me," she thought, her hand trembling slightly as she touched the delicate lace at her neckline.

Zelena had spent her life surviving, stealing to keep herself fed, and running from the dangers that threatened to consume her.

She'd never once imagined herself dressed like a lady, about to enter a world that had been denied to her for so long. For a moment, she hesitated. Would they see through her? Would they know that under the silk and the powder, she was still a runaway, someone who didn't belong?

The maids chattered excitedly as they added the final touches, but Zelena felt distant, as though she were watching someone else go through the motions. She tried to stand tall, to adopt the elegance that Lucien had insisted upon.

It was his world she was stepping into, after all. The man who had once been her captor was now her... what? Protector? Lover? That didn't quite fit, since they'd only kissed. She didn't know what to call him. He was the one who had chosen this dress, chosen this night, and chosen her.

When they arrived at the ball, Lucien had looked every bit the nobleman he was. His coat was a deep shade of blue, perfectly tailored to his broad frame. The cravat at his neck was tied just so, and his dark hair was brushed back, accentuating the sharp lines of his jaw.

He looked so polished, so powerful, and as she glanced at him from the corner of her eye, her stomach twisted with both nervousness and something else. Desire. She hated admitting it, but he excited her in ways no one ever had.

The carriage ride had been quiet, her heart pounding louder with each passing second. Upon their arrival at the grand estate, there was a noticeable shift in the air, laden with anticipation.

Lucien had stepped out first, his movements graceful and commanding. Then he turned and offered her his hand. She stared at it for a moment, knowing that once she took it, there would be no turning back.

Zelena hesitated as her foot hovered over the edge of the carriage, her heart racing. She could feel the eyes of the crowd already upon them. Whispers carried on through the night air.

For a moment, her confidence faltered. Could she do this? Could she truly step into this world and play the role of a lady?

Sensing her hesitation, Lucien's grip on her hand tightened ever so slightly, steadying her. His eyes met hers, a silent reassurance passing between them. She straightened her back, drawing in a deep breath, and stepped out.

The murmurs grew louder as they made their way toward the entrance. People were watching, of course they were. A Black woman, dressed as a lady, on the arm of a wealthy white man, it was scandalous, unheard of.

She could feel their eyes burning into her, some

with curiosity, others with outright disdain. But she lifted her chin and let Lucien guide her forward, even as her heart threatened to beat its way out of her chest. For a moment, everything else fell away.

The mansion loomed before her, its grand façade glowing in the evening light. As they stepped through the doors, she realized it wasn't the house or the people she feared anymore, but the way Lucien's hand on her arm made her feel more grounded than she'd ever been.

She walked in first, just as he'd instructed, her skirts sweeping the floor, her head held high. The sea of faces blurred together as the music from the ballroom floated toward her, a dizzying symphony of violins.

Zelena's pulse quickened, but she did not falter again. She was here. In this moment, she was more than she'd ever dared to dream.

The ballroom was a blur of silk gowns and polished shoes, the sound of music and laughter filling the air. She stood near the entrance, watching the glittering scene unfold before her like a dream.

Her heart raced, and she felt the impact of every eye in the room on her, though most were too absorbed in their own worlds to notice.

He appeared beside her, his presence grounding her amidst the whirlwind of emotions. "Nervous?"

She forced a smile, her voice steadier than she felt. "I've been through worse."

He chuckled softly, his eyes never leaving her face.

"You'll be fine. Just remember, head high, shoulders back. You've got this."

The words were simple, but they carried a weight of reassurance she hadn't expected. And so, with a deep breath, she stepped forward, entering the lion's den with her head held high.

The night was a blur of introductions, conversations, and subtle glances from women who noticed her, from men who tried to decipher who she was.

He had tried to dance with her, but she refused because she wasn't sure of herself. She didn't think the dance she knew would fit in with the elegant people.

At one point, he pulled her aside, leading her to the balcony where the cool night air kissed her flushed cheeks. They stood in silence for a moment, the sounds of the ball fading behind them.

"You did well tonight," he said, his voice low and approving.

"I barely made it through," she replied, shaking her head.

He turned to face her, his expression serious. "No, you did more than that. You proved you belong here."

Her eyes widened slightly. For so long, she had felt like an outsider, someone who didn't fit into this world of wealth and elegance. But tonight, something had shifted.

As the night drew to a close, they returned to the house in comfortable silence. She was tired, but there was a strange sense of fulfillment settling over her. She had faced the ball, and though it had been terrifying, she had come out the other side stronger.

Before she could retreat to her room, he caught her hand, stopping her in the dimly lit hallway.

"Wait."

She turned to face him, her heart suddenly in her throat.

He hesitated for a moment, as though choosing his words carefully. "I just wanted to say... I'm proud of you."

Her breath caught in her chest. No one had ever said that to her before, not in a way that felt real, anyway. The emotion in his eyes, the sincerity in his voice, it all made her feel... seen.

"I..." she started, unsure of how to respond. But instead of finishing her sentence, she stepped closer, her hand still in his.

For a moment, they stood like that, close, but not touching, the tension between them full of desire. The world faded away, leaving just the two of them in that quiet, intimate space.

And then, before she could second-guess herself, she leaned in, pressing her lips to his in a soft, tentative kiss. The moment their mouths touched, a jolt of electricity passed through her, igniting something deep within her.

Lucien froze for the briefest of moments, clearly taken aback by her boldness. But then, with a low groan, he responded. His arms wrapped around her, pulling her closer, and he kissed her back with fervor, all the restraint he'd been holding onto slipping away.

The kiss deepened, his lips moving over hers with a hunger that mirrored her own. They were lost in each other.

He wanted nothing more than to sweep her off her feet and carry her away, to take her to the privacy of his room and finally let the passion that had built between them consume them both.

His hands tightened around her waist, his body pressing against hers in a way that made his desires abundantly clear. Every fiber of him ached for her, and for a moment, he nearly gave in.

But then, just as suddenly as the kiss had started, Lucien pulled back. His breathing was ragged, his eyes dark with longing as they stared down at her.

His chest rose and plunged, and she could feel the raw energy vibrating between them. He wanted her, but he resisted once again, forcing himself to regain control.

"We can't," he whispered, though his voice was hoarse with emotion. "Not here. Not yet."

Zelena's heart pounded in her chest, her lips tingling from the kiss, but she nodded, understanding the weight of the situation. Still, as she looked up at him, she could see the battle he fought within himself, the war between his desire for her and the world they lived in.

She'd stirred something in him, something neither

of them could ignore, and she knew it was only a matter of time before they would.

The fire between them barely contained, but he was determined that she come to him, but not out of gratefulness..

CHAPTER-16

The first rays of sunlight filtered through the curtains, but she lay awake in bed, her thoughts racing. The kiss lingered in her mind, a sensation she couldn't shake. It had been brief, but it had shaken her to the core. *She knew she was too far gone.*

Her heart raced with uncertainty, and a part of her wanted to stay hidden under the covers, away from the reality she now had to face. There was no time to linger, however, because she had lessons to attend, duties to fulfill, and he would be waiting.

She rose, dressed carefully, and headed downstairs, her steps lighter than they had been in days.

As she approached the dining room, she hesitated just outside the door, hearing voices from within. It was him and Miss Everwood.

"She's improving quickly," Miss Everwood was

saying. "But there's still much to teach her if you want her to be ready."

"She's more than capable," he replied, his voice steady, though there was a warmth in his tone that made her heart skip. "I know she'll be ready."

Ready for what? She felt her pulse quicken and slowly stepped into the room, her entrance interrupting their conversation.

Both of them turned toward her, and for a moment, the air in the room seemed to still. He stood at the head of the table, his gaze locking onto hers, and she saw something flicker in his eyes, desire, but it was gone as quickly as it had appeared.

"Good morning," she said, trying to keep her voice even.

"Good morning," he replied, his expression unreadable. "We were just discussing your progress."

Miss Everwood smiled at her, offering a nod of approval. "You've come a long way. We'll continue working on conversation and etiquette, and then perhaps... we'll begin introducing you to some of the finer aspects of society."

She straightened herself and refused to let the pressure overwhelm her. "I'll do my best."

As the day wore on, she noticed the subtle distance from him. He had always been watchful, but now, there was a restraint in his actions, as though he was deliberately holding himself back.

She wondered about him more often than she cared

to admit. Who was he, really? Why had he chosen to bring her here, to teach her, to elevate her? The questions swirled in her mind, but she kept them to herself, knowing that asking would only complicate things.

The lessons continued, and Miss Everwood drilled her in every detail, from the proper way to address guests to the delicate art of maintaining a conversation without revealing too much. It wasn't just the lessons that occupied her thoughts.

Every time their eyes met, she felt the pull between them. It was like a storm brewing just beneath the surface, her surface especially, waiting for the right moment to break.

Later that evening, after hours of practicing with Miss Everwood, she took a moment to herself, stepping out into the garden for some fresh air. The night was cool, the stars twinkling above, and she breathed in deeply, savoring the quiet.

But she wasn't alone for long.

He appeared from the shadows, his presence unmistakable as he approached her. She turned to face him, her lips a crack open.

"I didn't mean to intrude on your conversation earlier," he said softly, his voice low and intimate in the garden's stillness. "I just… needed a moment."

She nodded, unsure of what to say. The space between them felt charged, the unspoken tension hanging thick in the air. For a long moment, neither of them spoke.

Finally, he broke the silence. "About last night…"

She froze. This was it, the moment she had been dreading and hoping for in equal measure.

"Last night," he continued, "was… unexpected. But I need you to understand something."

She braced herself, her heart pounding in her ears.

"You're important to me," he said, his eyes searching hers. "But I don't want you to feel like you owe me anything. What happened between us, what might happen, it has to be your choice."

Her eyes widened in surprise. Of all the things he could have said, she hadn't expected that.

He took a step closer, his gaze intense. "I don't want you to think that just because I'm teaching you, just because I've brought you into my world, that you're obligated to… to give me anything in return."

She blinked, trying to process his words. "I… I never thought that."

His shoulders relaxed slightly, as though her words had lifted a weight from him. "Good. Because the last thing I want is for you to feel trapped."

She shook her head, her voice soft. "I don't feel trapped. I just… I don't know what this is that I feel."

He stepped even closer, his hand reaching out to brush some stray hair away from her face. "Neither do I," he admitted, his voice barely above a whisper. "But I want to find out."

The lingering touch of his fingers against her skin had a profound effect on her, causing her to melt in his presence once more. The gap between them seemed to grow smaller, and with no hesitation, she instinctively moved closer, giving in to the warmth of his touch.

No, she didn't feel trapped at all.

The kiss that followed was slow, deliberate, nothing like the impulsive kiss from the night before. This time, there was no hesitation, no second-guessing. It was real, and it was mutual.

For a moment, the world fell away, leaving just the two of them in the quiet garden, the stars above bearing witness to their growing connection.

When they finally pulled apart, their breaths mingling in the cool night air, she felt a strange sense of peace settle over her. There was still so much uncertainty, so much that neither of them had said, but for the first time, she felt like they agreed, like they were both willing to see where this would go.

"I won't push you," he said softly, his hand still resting against her cheek. "But I won't pretend that I don't want more."

She smiled faintly, her heart full of emotions she hadn't expected. "I'm not sure what I want yet. But... I'm willing to try."

His eyes darkened with emotion, and he nodded, stepping back to give her space. "That's all I ask."

CHAPTER-17

◇◇◇

*S*he sat in the drawing room warmth nervously, awaiting her new tutor.

It had been a week since that night in the garden, and though she and he had shared stolen moments since, there had been no further discussions about their future.

Instead, he had clarified that her transformation into a lady was now a priority.

Her mind buzzed with uncertainty as she imagined what this tutor might be like. Would they be as harsh as Miss Everwood? Would they offer the same quiet understanding she had shown her?

The door creaked open, and a tall, slender man with a stern expression walked in. His attire was impeccable, his spectacles perched perfectly on his nose. His cold, appraising eyes swept over her, making her feel small in her seat.

He bowed slightly. "Miss, I am Mr. Abernathy. I will instruct you in language, etiquette, and proper social conduct."

His voice was smooth, but carried a weight of authority that sent a chill down her spine. She could feel the challenge in his tone, as if he were daring her to fail.

"I'll try my best," she replied, her voice small but steady.

The lessons began immediately, and it quickly became apparent that Mr. Abernathy would tolerate nothing less than perfection. He corrected her pronunciation relentlessly, forced her to recite complex phrases, and drilled her on everything from posture to proper greetings.

Compared to him, Miss Lillian was a rookie. Each misstep felt like a small defeat, and by the end of the day, her body ached, and her mind was weary.

He watched from a distance, his expression unreadable, as Mr. Abernathy scolded her for a minor mistake in her grammar. There was no comfort, no softness in the way the tutor handled her, but it was clear it was necessary.

She hated it. Every word she stumbled over, every correction, felt like a strike against her pride. But more than that, she hated feeling weak in front of him.

The man who had kissed her under the stars now watched her struggle to become something she wasn't sure she could be. She had prided herself on her progress, but it was clear she had a long way to go. A very long way.

Days turned into weeks, and the pressure mounted. Every lesson felt like a battlefield, and every evening she found herself more exhausted than the last.

Mr. Abernathy's patience wore thin with her defiance, though she could see that he took some strange satisfaction in breaking her down, bit by bit.

One afternoon, after yet another grueling session, she snapped.

"I ain't no lady," she spat, her voice raw with frustration that made her revert to the way she spoke originally. "It doesn't matter how many words you throw at me. I ain't never gonna talk like them rich folk."

Mr. Abernathy's eyes narrowed, his lips pursing in disapproval. "If you cannot adapt, Miss Zelena, then you are simply wasting everyone's time."

She wasn't good enough, not for Mr. Abernathy, not for society, and maybe never for Lucien. The tears stung at the back of her eyes, but she refused to let them fall. She would not give Mr. Abernathy the satisfaction of seeing her break.

As her anger rose, so did her determination. She had survived too much to let this man, or anyone else, tell her what she couldn't be.

She took a deep breath, steadying herself. "I'll do it. I'll learn it all. But I'll do it my way."

That evening, she found herself alone with him for the first time in days. He had watched her fiery exchange with Mr. Abernathy from the shadows, his face unreadable, as always.

"I heard about today," he said softly, stepping into the room, the warmth of the fire casting flickering shadows across his face.

Her heart skipped a beat, and she straightened her back, refusing to show any weakness. "Yeah, well... I am not giving up, no matter how hard that man tries to make me."

He smiled faintly, stepping closer until the warmth of his body seemed to radiate toward her. "I never doubted you."

His words were simple, but they filled her with a quiet strength. For a moment, she saw the man who had kissed her under the stars, the man who had stopped his henchmen from hurting her that fateful day when they'd met.

But there was still so much unsaid between them.

CHAPTER-18

*W*eeks had passed since her fiery exchange with Mr. Abernathy, and though the lessons remained as grueling as ever, something had changed within her.

She had approached each challenge not with frustration, but with determination. Her speech grew less rough, her posture more poised, though it was still a struggle to fight the habits she'd carried for so long.

The mornings were filled with endless repetition, words, phrases, gestures that felt foreign to her, but she pushed through, if only to prove to herself that she could.

One afternoon, as she practiced with Mr. Abernathy, she noticed her sentences flowed smoother. She no longer stumbled over words, and her manners, though not perfect, were showing promise.

Her biggest realization came when she caught herself correcting her own speech without thinking.

Her pride at this minor victory was short-lived when Mr. Abernathy gave a curt nod, his version of approval. "Better," he said dryly, moving on to the next exercise.

But in her heart, she knew she was finally starting to change.

LATER THAT WEEK, she was summoned to the ballroom. A place she had only ever cleaned before, now transformed into a practice ground for her etiquette lessons.

The grandeur of the room, with its gilded walls and shimmering chandeliers, was intimidating.

She entered cautiously, her eyes sweeping over the opulence. The dress she wore, one of the fine garments he had provided, felt strange on her body, constricting and delicate in ways she wasn't used to.

He stood near the window, waiting for her. When he turned to face her, his eyes swept over her form with a subtle appreciation, though he said nothing. Instead, he stepped forward, offering his hand in a silent invitation to dance.

Her pulse quickened, not out of fear, but out of a nervous anticipation. She had never danced before, not in a way that fit the world he came from.

The closest she'd come to it was swaying in the shadows of dimly lit taverns, moving to the rhythm of drunken fiddles.

She hesitated before slipping her hand into his.

"We'll go slow," he said softly, guiding her toward the center of the room. His grip was firm yet gentle, and the warmth of his hand seemed to seep through her skin, making her acutely aware of every movement.

As they moved, the distance between them lessened, their bodies fitting together more naturally than she expected. She tried to follow his lead, awkwardly at first, but as the minutes passed, she eased into the steps. The soft music swirled around them, and for the first time in weeks, she felt almost graceful.

But even as she focused on her footing, her mind wandered to him and the way he held her, the intensity of his gaze. It was more than a lesson. There was a tenderness in the way he touched her, something that went beyond the surface.

As the dance drew to a close, they remained standing close, their breaths slightly uneven from the effort. He didn't release her hand immediately, holding her gaze instead.

"You're improving," he said softly, his voice low and hushed, as if they were sharing a secret. "You've come a long way."

She looked up at him, her chest tightening with a mix of pride and uncertainty. "It's difficult," she whispered. "This world... it's difficult to belong here."

He stepped closer, his hand lifting her chin up. "You belong wherever you choose to be."

Her breath caught at the warmth of his touch. For the first time in weeks, she felt a sense of hope that maybe, just maybe, he was right. But there was still a part of her that couldn't believe it.

"I don't even know who I am anymore," she admitted, her voice barely above a whisper. "All these lessons... all this change... it's like I'm losing myself."

He frowned, his hand stilling against her cheek. "You're not losing yourself. You're becoming more of who you're meant to be."

There was an intensity in his words that made her heart skip. He saw something in her, something she hadn't seen in herself for so long. But more than that, he was giving her the chance to find it.

"What if I don't want this?" she asked, her voice shaking. "What if I can't ever be the woman you want me to be?"

His eyes softened, and he stepped closer until their bodies were almost touching. "I don't want you to be anything you're not. I only want you to be who you are... whoever that may be."

His words settled deep within her, filling the empty spaces that had been carved out by years of struggle and survival. For the first time in her life, she felt seen, truly understood, and it terrified her, but it also gave her a strange sense of freedom.

Over the next few days, their lessons became a dance of their own, each moment filled with unspoken emotions.

He would watch her during her tutoring sessions, his eyes tracing her movements as if trying to decipher the person she was becoming. And in return, she would catch herself glancing at him more often, wondering where it would all lead to, even though she already knew.

One evening, after an exhausting day of lessons, she found herself standing outside on the veranda, gazing out at the estate's sprawling gardens.

The cool night air brushed against her skin, and she wrapped her arms around herself, lost in thought.

She didn't hear him approach until he was standing beside her.

"Can't sleep?" he asked quietly.

She shook her head; her gaze still focused on the moonlit gardens. "Too much to think about."

There was a long pause before he spoke again. "You don't have to do this, you know. If it's too much—"

"No," she interrupted, her voice firm. "I want this. I want to... I want to be better."

He turned to face her, his expression softening. "You're already better."

Her heart fluttered at his words, and she allowed herself to believe them. There was still so much she didn't understand, about him, about herself, about what the future held for them.

"I don't know what's gonna happen," she whispered, finally looking up at him. "But I want to try."

His gaze was intense. "So do I."

CHAPTER-19

The following morning, the air in the estate felt different. There was a tension that had not been there before.

When she stepped into the dining room to serve breakfast, the usual calm was disrupted by hushed voices and furtive glances between the servants.

She knew immediately that something had changed.

It wasn't long before she found out why.

"They're comin' for him," whispered one maid as they passed in the hallway.

"What?" she asked, her heart tightening.

"Mr. — people are talkin'. They say he's been too soft, takin' in someone like you. They're watchin' him now."

Her stomach dropped. The walls of the house, once a shelter, now felt like they were closing in.

She had always known the peace couldn't last forever, but she hadn't expected it to unravel so quickly. She couldn't find him anywhere in the house and she was worried about him.

Later in the day, he found her in the study, where she had been dusting shelves to keep herself occupied. His face was set, his expression tight. There was no trace of the tenderness from their last encounter.

"I've been called to a meeting," he said, his voice low, controlled. "They want me to explain why you're still here."

Her hands froze on the duster. She swallowed, trying to keep her voice steady. "So, what're you going to do?"

He sighed, running a hand through his hair in frustration. "What can I do? They're pressuring me, questioning my decisions. They think I've... lost control."

She bristled, feeling a familiar anger rise within her. "Because of me?"

"No," he said sharply, stepping closer. "Because they're narrow-minded. They think everything has to fit into their little world of rules and traditions."

"So what happens now?" she asked, her voice quieter.

He looked at her for a long moment, his gaze unreadable. "I'll fight them. But you have to be careful and stay here. They'll try to use you to get to me."

For the next few days, the tension in the estate only

grew. The once easy banter between them was replaced with silence, not out of anger, but out of caution. The world outside was pressing in on them, and it was affecting everything.

One afternoon, as she practiced her reading with Mr. Abernathy, her thoughts drifted to him. She hadn't seen him much since their conversation in the study, and she could feel the distance between them widening.

It gnawed at her, the uncertainty of their future together.

That evening, she found herself in the library again, pacing restlessly by the window. She was about to leave when she heard the door creak open behind her.

He stepped in, his face weary, as if he'd been carrying a heavy load all day. Without a word, he crossed the room and stood by the fireplace, staring into the flames.

"I've been thinking," she said, her voice cutting through the silence. "Maybe... maybe I shouldn't be here anymore."

His head snapped up, eyes flashing with surprise and something close to pain. "What are you saying?"

"I mean... you're risking everything for me. Maybe it's not worth it."

He moved toward her, closing the distance between them in a few quick strides. "It's worth it," he said, his voice firm. "Don't you see? You're worth it."

She shook her head, her emotions rising to the surface. "But what if, what if they win? What if they take you down because of me?"

"They won't," he said fiercely. "Because I won't let them."

The intensity in his eyes was undeniable, but she wasn't convinced. "I don't want to be the reason you lose everything."

He cupped her face gently, forcing her to meet his gaze. "You won't be. I told you before, you belong here, wherever you choose to be. And I want you here. With me."

Her heart ached at his words, the sincerity in his voice. She had never felt this way before, wanted. Nonetheless, the fear of losing it all lingered in the back of her mind.

"I'm scared," she whispered, her voice trembling.

"So am I," he admitted, his thumb brushing against her cheek. "But we'll face it together. If you'll let me."

Without warning, he leaned down, capturing her lips in a kiss that was soft at first, then deepened with all the emotions they had both been holding back.

It wasn't a kiss of desperation or fear but one of promise, a vow that whatever happened, they would face it head-on, and together.

When they finally pulled apart, their breaths ragged, he pressed his forehead against hers. "Stay with me," he whispered.

Her heart raced, but for the first time, her stomach settled because he'd decided and chosen her. She didn't feel the urge to run, anyway, because she wanted to be with him. Instead, she nodded, her hands tightening around his. "I will."

CHAPTER-20

*a*s the days passed, the tension surrounding the estate grew heavier, like a storm building on the horizon.

The once peaceful house now felt more like a fortress under siege, with every glance and hushed conversation from the staff reminding her that danger was lurking just beyond the walls.

Her lessons with Mr. Abernathy continued, though the impact of their new reality hung over every word she struggled to read. She could sense the shift in the household dynamics, even if no one spoke of it directly.

The servants were wary, more careful in their interactions with her because they felt she was at risk, as was their entire world.

But Lucien was her anchor in the growing chaos

with his steady presence, and his resolve clear, though she could see the toll it was taking on him.

She had never known him to look so exhausted, shadows darkening beneath his eyes, his movements heavier, more deliberate.

One evening, after everyone else had retired, she wandered the halls, restless. She knew what was coming, knew that the people in town would not let this situation continue much longer without forcing a confrontation.

The whispers about him had grown louder, the disapproval more vocal, and it was all because of her.

Late that night, as she slipped through the back of the house, she overheard something that stopped her in her tracks.

A group of men, his trusted advisors, were meeting in the drawing room, speaking in low, urgent tones. She pressed herself against the wall, straining to hear.

"We can't protect him much longer," one of the voices said, the words sharp. "He's putting everything at risk for that girl."

"You know how they talk in town. They're saying he's lost his mind."

"I've been approached by several of the wealthiest families. They want answers and action."

Her heart pounded as she realized the extent of the pressure he was under. These men weren't just voicing concerns, they were planning something, plotting to push him into a corner.

"We'll have to confront him soon. Before it's too late. Our livelihoods are at stake too."

As the voices faded and the men moved on, she stayed hidden, her thoughts racing. They were right that he was putting everything on the line for her, and she was terrified that if it came down to it, she wouldn't be enough to keep him safe.

He found her sitting by the window in the library, her knees drawn up to her chest as she stared out at the darkened grounds. She didn't hear him enter, didn't know he was there until he gently placed a hand on her shoulder.

"You're not sleeping," he said softly.

She shook her head, unable to meet his gaze. "Neither are you."

He sighed, pulling up a chair beside her. "It's... tough right now."

She laughed bitterly, wiping at her eyes. "Difficult doesn't even cover it."

They remained silent for a few moments, allowing the magnitude of their unspoken fears to fill the tense atmosphere.

"I heard them," she finally whispered. "Your men. They're going to push you out. Because of me."

"They won't," he said, his voice calm but firm.

"They will." She turned to face him, her eyes blazing with emotion. "Don't you see? I'm the problem. If I wasn't here, none of this would be happening."

His hand tightened around hers. "You're not leaving."

"You can't protect me forever," she said, her voice breaking. "You're risking everything."

"I'm risking nothing compared to what you've given up to be here," he said fiercely. "And I'm not letting you go. Not now. Not ever."

The next day, Lucien made a bold decision. Knowing that whispers were growing louder and threats were inching closer, he called for a gathering of the estate's workers and advisors.

It was a calculated move, one meant to show that he would not be swayed by fear or pressure.

She watched from the edges of the courtyard as he stood before them, addressing the group with a calm authority that commanded respect.

He spoke of loyalty, of the values that his family had always upheld, of the importance of standing firm in the face of adversity.

And then, in a move that shocked everyone, he took her hand and brought her to stand beside him.

There was a collective gasp from the crowd as they looked at her, standing with him as an equal, not as a servant or a mere woman, to be dismissed. He had claimed her, not just privately, but publicly.

"You all know who she is," he said, his voice ringing out across the courtyard. "And you know what she means to me. I will not hide her. I will not send her away. If any man here cannot accept that, he is free to leave."

The silence that followed was deafening, the tension almost unbearable. But no one moved, and no one dared challenge him.

When the day was ending, she stumbled upon him in his study, observing his drooping shoulders.

She approached him quietly, unsure of what to say. He had put everything on the line for her today, and she wasn't sure she could ever repay him for that.

"You didn't have to do that," she whispered, standing in the doorway.

He looked up, his eyes tired but resolute. "Yes, I did."

She stepped closer, feeling the pull between them stronger than ever. "Why? Why take such a risk for me? You have a lot to lose. "

He stood, crossing the room to stand in front of her. "Because I believe in you. In us."

Her heart stopped as he took her hands in his, his gaze unwavering. "You're not just a woman I took in. You're everything I never knew I needed."

Swallowing hard, she could feel her heart racing inside her chest, overwhelmed by the intensity of the moment. "What if it's not enough? What if they come for us?"

"Then we'll face them together," he said, his voice low but certain. "As long as you're with me."

As her emotions took over, she nodded, unable to contain them. She had never felt so afraid, and yet, so safe.

He was risking everything for her, and for the first time, she realized just how much she would fight for that life, that love they'd built.

CHAPTER-21

The ripples from his public declaration the day before spread quickly.

By morning, everyone in the surrounding towns knew what had happened, how he had openly defended her, a woman of questionable standing, against the powerful families who had been pressuring him.

He had drawn a line in the sand, and now the consequences were closing in.

The atmosphere during breakfast at the estate was thick with a sense of excitement and anticipation. The servants moved quietly, casting furtive glances toward her.

She could feel the tension, but it was no longer directed solely at her. The significance of what lay ahead was burdensome for all of them to bear.

He entered the room, his face as composed as ever,

but she could see the strain etched in the lines around his eyes.

Sitting beside her at the table, he gave her a reassuring look, but it wasn't enough to ease the gnawing dread in her chest.

"They'll come," he mumbled as they ate. "But we'll be ready."

She nodded, trying to push away the fear. She wasn't used to people fighting for her like this, and it terrified her how much she depended on him, how much she wanted this life with him.

Later in the day, he left the estate to meet with some of the prominent figures in town. Though he didn't say it aloud, she knew it was an effort to make peace before things escalated further.

As much as he wanted to protect her, he couldn't simply ignore the power these families held.

As he rode into town, she watched from the window, her heart heavy with worry. What if they demanded he make a choice between her and his position? What if he was forced to give up everything because of her?

Her thoughts spiraled as the day wore on, the tension unbearable. She paced the halls, unable to focus on anything else. When he finally returned that evening, his face was grave.

"They're not backing down," he said, his voice low as he sat in the drawing room with her. "The request has been made for me to put an end to this... arrangement. They say I've shamed my family."

Her chest tightened. "And what did you say?"

"I told them I wouldn't be bullied. I won't let them dictate my life." His words were firm, but there was a flicker of doubt in his eyes, just for a moment, and she saw it.

She stood, crossing the room to him, her hands trembling as she reached out to touch his arm. "You don't have to do this. You don't have to fight them for me."

He looked up at her, his gaze intense. "I want to. Don't you understand? This is my choice."

She shook her head; the fear bubbling to the surface. "But what if you lose everything? What if they take everything from you?"

"Then I'll start again," he said softly, his hand closing over hers. "But I won't lose you."

There was nothing more to be said.

The following morning, a group of men arrived at the estate. They were the same men who had advised him for years, powerful allies who had now turned against him, their influence over the town and its affairs undeniable.

She watched from a distance as they gathered in his study, their voices low but filled with tension.

She couldn't hear the conversation, but she didn't need to. She knew what they were saying, warning him of the consequences if he didn't end things with her, urging him to see reason. It felt like her very presence was the fuse to a powder keg, one that could explode at any moment.

After what felt like hours, the men finally left, their faces grim as they passed by her without so much as a glance. She waited in the hall, her heart pounding as he emerged from the study, his expression unreadable.

"They've given me an ultimatum," he said, his voice quiet but steady. "I either send you away, or they'll cut off all support. Financially, politically, socially. I'll lose everything."

Her throat tightened, her worst fears realized. "And what are you going to do?"

He looked at her for a long moment, his eyes filled with a mixture of sadness and resolve. "I'm going to stand by you."

Tears welled up in her eyes, but she quickly blinked them away. "You don't have to do this," she whispered. "You could send me away. I'd understand."

"No," he said firmly, stepping closer. "We've come too far for that. I won't let them win. I won't let them take you from me. There comes a time in life when one has to make a stand."

That night, after the tension of the day had settled into an uneasy silence, they found themselves alone in the library. He was seated by the fire, staring into the flames, lost in thought.

She hesitated at the door, unsure of what to say. She had never been good with words, not like the ladies in his world who could spin pretty phrases and soothe men's troubled hearts.

She, however, knew she couldn't leave him alone in this because he had risked everything for her, and she needed to show him she understood what that meant.

Quietly, she walked over and knelt beside his chair, placing a hand on his knee. He looked down at her, his expression softening as their eyes met.

"I don't know how to thank you for what you're

doing," she said, her voice trembling. "I've never had someone fight for me like this, especially when I don't think I deserve it."

He frowned, reaching out to cup her cheek. "You deserve everything, and I don't want you to doubt that."

Her heart swelled at his words, but the fear still lingered. "I just... I'm scared of what's coming and of what they'll do."

"So am I," he admitted quietly. "But we'll face it together. Whatever happens."

The next morning, they received a letter. It was from one of the wealthiest families in the area, a family whose support he had relied on for years. The letter was formal, but the message was clear: they were severing ties with him. He was being cast out of their social circle, his business interests threatened, his reputation tarnished.

He read the letter in silence, his face unreadable, before passing it to her. She read the words, her heart sinking as the full weight of what this meant settled over her.

"They've started," he said quietly. "The others will follow."

Her hands trembled as she set the letter down. "I'm so sorry."

He shook his head, his eyes hardening with determination. "Don't be. This was always coming and now we know who our enemies are."

CHAPTER-22

*W*ord spread quickly, and the isolation they feared became a reality. By the end of the week, invitations to social gatherings for him were no longer extended, business contracts were quietly rescinded, and once-loyal allies now turned their backs on him.

His name, once respected, was now whispered with contempt in the parlors of the town's elite.

Inside the estate, the atmosphere shifted. The servants were loyal but cautious, sensing the tension in the air.

Fewer visitors came, and the once-lively halls were now silent, save for the quiet moments they shared in the solitude of their home.

One afternoon, she found him in his study, staring at the letters piled high on his desk, formal rejections, notices of contracts ended, and social invitations that had evaporated.

His business, his reputation, his entire standing in society were slipping away.

For a long moment, she stood in the doorway, watching him. He was always so composed, so controlled. But now, she could see the strain on his face due to all his troubles.

She stepped forward quietly, her voice barely a whisper. "You could still let me go because it's not too late." She loved him enough to let him go.

He looked up sharply, his eyes darkening. "I'm not sending you away."

"But this is costing you everything," she insisted, her voice trembling with the emotion she had been holding back for days. "It's not fair for you to lose everything because of me."

He stood, crossing the room to stand in front of her. "I told you before that this is my choice. I would lose a thousand times more if I let you go. Don't ask me to do that."

Tears filled her eyes, but she swallowed them back. "I just don't want to see you suffer because of me."

His gaze softened as he reached out to cup her face. "You are not the cause of my suffering. You are the reason I'm still fighting."

Despite his determination, the reality of their burden weighed heavily on both of them.

Away from prying eyes, their connection deepened,

and they formed an unspoken bond that strengthened as they faced adversity together. Beyond the confines of the estate, the pressure continued to build.

Not all within his household were as loyal as they appeared. Some of the staff, fearful of losing their own positions and reputations, began whispering about her. She overheard fragments of their conversations, servants questioning why he was risking everything for "a girl like her," wondering if it was worth it.

The words stung, but she kept her head high. She couldn't blame them because if things continued the way they were going, they would lose their jobs and the life they knew.

Because of their status as slaves, there was always the risk of being sold to brutal masters, or worse. She knew they saw her as an outsider, someone who didn't belong in his world.

They were right; she didn't belong with them but yet didn't belong with Lucien's class either. They didn't see was how much she had changed since her arrival. She wasn't the same woman who had stolen to survive, who had walked into his life with nothing but defiance and fear.

She had learned and grown and was becoming more than she had ever thought possible. The judgment from all sides lingered like a shadow.

Their relationship had grown stronger in some ways, but the strain showed in others. He was away more often, trying to salvage what he could of his business and reputation.

She found herself alone in the vast estate, unable to talk with anyone, her thoughts spiraling as the isolation deepened.

One evening, after another long day of silence, she confronted him when he returned.

"You're slipping away from me," she said, her voice breaking.

He looked at her, weary but determined. "I'm trying to protect what we have."

"But you're barely here anymore," she replied, the frustration and fear she had kept hidden finally boiling over. "It's all about the business, about the reputation. I care about you and about us, but I see you looking and feeling worse."

He sighed, running a hand through his hair. "I'm trying to hold it all together."

"I don't need it all," she said, stepping closer. "I just need you and I don't want to lose you to this... fight."

As his eyes softened, a fleeting moment passed where the burden of everything seemed to evaporate. He took her hand, pulling her close. "You won't lose me. I promise you that."

The promises were harder to keep as the weeks dragged on. The external pressure continued to mount, and cracks formed in the foundation of their relationship.

It happened late one night. He had been distant for days, and she couldn't take it anymore. She found him in the study, buried in paperwork, trying to salvage what was left of his crumbling empire.

"I can't do this," she blurted out, her voice sharp with frustration. "I can't sit here and watch you destroy yourself for something that doesn't even matter."

He looked up, his expression hardening. "It does matter."

"Why? Because of them?" she shot back, gesturing to the letters piled on his desk. "Because of what they think? What they want from you?"

"This is my life," he said, his voice rising. "This is everything I've built."

"And what about me?" she demanded, her voice

trembling. "What about us? You're losing me in this... fight for something that you're already losing."

He slammed his hand on the desk, his anger flashing for the first time. "You think I don't know that? You think I'm not trying to protect us both?"

"Protecting us from what?" she shot back, her voice cracking. "From them? From yourself?"

There was a long, heavy silence. He stared at her, his chest heaving, his fists clenched. She could see the battle in his eyes, the war between the man he wanted to be for her and the man the world was forcing him to become.

"I love you," he finally said, his voice hoarse. "But I can't lose everything I've worked for, that my family has worked for."

"And I love you," she whispered, her heart breaking. "But I'm afraid if you keep fighting this fight, you'll lose me, anyway."

How could she convince him it was best to look for other ways to survive? He was essentially wasting his time because his former allies had already made their decision, rendering his efforts pointless.

CHAPTER-23

The atmosphere became charged with unexpressed emotions and unresolved strain after their explosive argument.

Days passed without either of them addressing the conflict, and though they still shared the same space, it felt as if an invisible wall had risen between them.

The once easy companionship, the spark that had drawn them together, was clouded by the strain of everything left unsaid.

He buried himself in work, determined to save what little was left of his reputation. She spent her days lost in thought, questioning whether she truly belonged in this world he was so desperate to cling to.

One evening, she wandered through the estate's garden as she often did. The night was quiet, the air still and heavy. She paused by the fountain, her reflection shimmering on the surface of the water. For the first time since their argument, the enormity of the situation truly hit her.

Was this what her life had become? A battle between who she was and who she was expected to be? She had fought so hard to survive on her own, to maintain her independence, but now she was caught in a world that declared her unfit for its mold.

She didn't hear him approach, but suddenly, he was there, standing just behind her. They sat in silence for a moment, and then he mustered the courage to speak up, breaking the stillness.

"I miss you," he finally said, his voice soft but filled with a raw emotion she hadn't heard in days.

Her throat tightened. "I'm still here."

"No, you're not," he said, stepping closer, his hand brushing lightly against her shoulder. "Not really."

She turned to face him, her eyes filled with tears she couldn't hold back any longer. "And where are you? Buried in work, trying to hold on to a world that's slipping away? Or standing here with me?"

For a moment, the tension broke, and he pulled her into his arms. The warmth of his embrace, the familiar scent of him, made her heart ache. She had missed that, missed him, but she didn't know how to bridge the gap that had grown between them.

"I'm scared," he admitted quietly, his voice barely audible. "I've never been this scared before."

Her breath caught in her throat as she pulled back to look at him, her eyes searching his. It was rare for him to admit weakness, to show the fear he tried so hard to hide beneath his confidence.

"You fear losing everything you've built," she whispered, uttering for the first time out loud what he had been feeling for so long.

He shook his head. "No. I fear losing you."

The confession hit her like a wave, washing over her in a flood of emotion. She had thought his obsession with his reputation had driven them apart, but now she realized it was more than that. He was afraid that in fighting for her, he would lose her.

"I'm not going anywhere," she whispered, her fingers gently brushing against his cheek. "But I need you to meet me halfway."

His eyes softened, and for a long moment, they simply stood there, wrapped in each other's presence. "I don't know how to fix this," he admitted, his voice laced with desperation. "Everything is falling apart around us."

"Then let it," she said, her voice stronger than she felt. "Let it all fall apart, because none of it matters if we're not standing together when it's over."

He pulled her close again, his arms tightening around her as if he were afraid to let her go. The wall between them broke, and she dared to believe they could accept their fate.

"I'll fight for us," he said, his voice firm but filled with tenderness. "I'll fight, but I can't do it alone."

"You won't have to," she promised, her head resting against his chest. "We'll face it together."

As the days passed, they rebuilt what had been broken. It wasn't easy. There were still moments of doubt, of fear. He pulled away from the business deals that had consumed him, spending more time with her, talking through the fears that had once kept them apart.

She threw herself into her lessons with renewed focus. If she was to truly become a part of his world, she needed to embrace the changes, not fight them.

This time, it wasn't about losing herself but about being both the woman she had been and the woman she was becoming.

Even as they strengthened their bond, a new challenge loomed on the horizon. Rumors swirled in town, whispers of scandal that reached even the highest echelons of society. His enemies, sensing weakness, closed in, and they knew their fight was far from over. They were barely hanging on as it was. He would have to consider letting some of his staff go.

One evening, as they sat together by the fire, he brought up a letter he had received earlier that day.

"We've been invited to a gala," he said, his tone cautious. "It's a chance for us to show everyone that nothing has changed, that we're still... together and united."

She looked at him, her brow furrowing. "And you think this will help?"

"I don't know," he admitted. "But it's the first time we've been invited to anything since all of this started. It's a step."

She bit her lip, uncertainty gnawing at her. "And you want me to go? To be... paraded around like a trophy?"

He reached for her hand, his gaze steady. "I want you to be by my side. I want them to see that we're in this together."

With a heavy heart, she gazed downwards at their hands entwined together. "It won't be easy."

"I know," he said softly. "But we're stronger together, aren't we?"

She met his gaze, her resolve hardening. "Yes. We are."

CHAPTER-24

The night of the gala arrived faster than either of them expected. For her, the day had been a whirlwind of preparations, hours spent with her teacher reviewing every detail, every etiquette rule, every phrase she might need to avoid humiliation.

Despite all the progress she had made, she felt an overwhelming sense of dread. Could she really pull it off?

He had reassured her countless times that she didn't have to be perfect, that just being herself was enough. In her heart, she knew it wasn't about her anymore, but about them.

It was about proving that their relationship was more than just a passing affair, that she belonged in his world.

As she stood before the mirror in her elegant gown, she hardly recognized herself. The once rough, defiant woman who had survived by her wits now looked like a lady of high society.

Beneath the polished exterior, the fire still burned. She had never been one to let others decide her worth, and tonight wouldn't be any different.

He approached her from behind, his hands gently resting on her shoulders as he looked at her reflection in the mirror. "You look stunning."

She smiled, but it didn't reach her eyes. "Do you really think they'll accept me?"

He pressed a kiss to the top of her head, his voice low and steady. "I don't care if they do. You're with me, and that's all that matters."

She turned to face him, her fingers brushing lightly against his chest. "You know it's not just about us, is it? It never has been."

He paused, his expression softening. "No. It hasn't. But tonight, we show them they don't get to decide our future."

The carriage ride to the gala was quiet, the tension apparent despite their shared resolve. As they pulled up to the grand estate where the event was being held, she felt her heart race. With its bright lights, the building loomed large and dominated the landscape.

When they stepped out, all eyes turned toward them. The whispers started almost immediately, a wave of murmurs sweeping through the crowd.

She could feel the weight of their gazes, the judgment in their stares. It was even worse than her first gala with him, but she held her head high, determined not to let them see her fear.

He offered his arm, and she took it, walking beside him as if she belonged in this world. She would not let them win.

Inside, the room was filled with the glittering elite of society. Women in extravagant gowns and men in tailored suits milled about, laughing and chatting as if nothing in the world could disturb their carefully constructed bubbles of privilege.

They hadn't been in the room for more than a few moments when a man approached, someone she recognized from the whispers, a powerful business owner who had once been one of her Lucien's allies.

His eyes flicked to her, and though his smile was polite, she could see the disdain in his gaze.

"It's been a while," the man said, his tone dripping with insincerity. "I hear you've been keeping... interesting company."

Lucien's jaw tightened, but he didn't let the slight go unanswered. "We've all had to make adjustments lately. I'm sure you understand."

The man chuckled, but there was no warmth in it. "Oh, I understand perfectly." His gaze shifted to her again, his smile widening. "And how are you finding our little society, my dear? Overwhelming, I imagine?"

She met his gaze, her chin lifting slightly. "I've survived worse."

The man's smile faltered for just a moment,

surprised by her defiance, but then he recovered, nodding slightly before turning his attention back to her Lucien. "Well, I hope you both enjoy yourselves tonight. I'm sure it will be... memorable."

As the evening progressed, she stayed aware of the stares and whispers that followed her. People had mixed reactions to her, some disapproving, but others were curious and wanted to learn more about the woman who had won his love.

Finally, as the night wore on, he pulled her onto the dance floor. The room seemed to fade away as they moved together, his hand on the small of her back guiding her through the steps.

"You're doing beautifully," he whispered, his breath warm against her ear.

She smiled up at him, the tension in her chest loosening just a little. "I feel like I'm drowning in judgment."

"Let them judge," he said softly, his eyes never leaving hers. "They're just scared because they know they could never be as brave as you."

She leaned into him, her heart swelling with a mixture of fear and pride. He had always known exactly what to say to make her feel strong, even when she doubted herself.

But the night wasn't over yet.

As the music swelled and the dance came to a close, a woman approached them. She was stunning, draped in silk and jewels, with a sharp smile that didn't quite reach her eyes.

"I must say," the woman began, her tone dripping with condescension, "you've certainly made an impression tonight. It's not every day we get to see someone so... unique gracing our halls."

Lucien tensed beside her, but before he could speak, she stepped forward. "Thank you. I suppose I'm just full of surprises."

The woman's smile faltered, her eyes narrowing slightly. "Indeed. But tell me, how do you plan to keep up? Surely this world must feel so... foreign to someone like you."

The implication was clear. She didn't belong here, and everyone knew it. But instead of shrinking under the weight of the insult, she smiled, her voice calm and measured.

"I've always been good at adapting, and one thing I know for sure is that change is coming. You either adapt or die," she said, her gaze steady. "Besides, I have an excellent teacher."

Lucien squeezed her hand, pride shining in his eyes. The woman, clearly flustered, gave a tight smile before turning on her heel and walking away.

"You were incredible," he whispered as they sat side by side in the carriage, the quiet of the night a stark contrast to the buzz of the gala.

She looked over at him, her heart still racing from

the confrontation. "I don't know if I can do this... if I can keep facing people like that."

"You couldn't have handled it better," he reminded her, his hand finding hers.

She leaned her head against his shoulder, exhaustion creeping in. "I just hope it's enough."

"It will be," he said with quiet certainty. "You're stronger than you know."

As the carriage pulled away from the grand estate, she felt a small flicker of hope. Maybe they would survive this after-all.

They had invited them to humiliate them, but they had been shocked by their defiance. It was a small win for them, but a win nonetheless.

CHAPTER-25

The next morning, the reactions of the previous night still hung in the air as they sat in the drawing room.

She recollected the feeling of all the eyes that had been on her, judging her every move. Every word she spoke, every gesture she made, it all seemed under scrutiny.

He sat across from her, looking over some papers, though his focus was clearly elsewhere. "I think last night went better than expected," he said, attempting to break the silence.

She arched an eyebrow, her skepticism obvious. "Better than expected? I could feel their hatred. You saw the way they looked at me."

He leaned forward, setting his papers down. "Yes, I did. But I also saw someone very important take notice of you."

She frowned, confused. "What are you talking about?"

He gave a small, knowing smile. "Baroness DeClark."

Her heart skipped a beat at the name. The Baroness was one of the most influential women in their social circle and her approval could sway even the coldest hearts. Why, though, would someone like her even take notice?

"She came up to me after you spoke with that woman last night," he explained. "She asked who you were."

Her stomach tightened. "And what did you tell her?"

"I told her the truth," he said, his voice calm. "That you're the strongest, most incredible woman I've ever met. And that I intend to spend the rest of my life with you."

She blinked, momentarily stunned by his words. He had never spoken so directly about their future before.

"What did she say?" she asked, her voice barely above a whisper.

"She smiled," he said, leaning back in his chair. "And she said, 'She's quite something, isn't she? I look forward to seeing her again.'"

Later that afternoon, as they sat together in the library, a knock came at the door. One housemaid entered, holding a small, elegant envelope. It was addressed to her.

She opened it with trembling hands, unsure of what

to expect. Inside was an invitation, handwritten in the Baroness's elegant script, inviting her to a private tea at the Baroness's estate the following week.

Her eyes widened as she read the invitation, her mind racing. This was more than just a social call; it was a signal. A signal that perhaps things might be changing.

"What does it say?" he asked, observing her.

She handed him the invitation, too stunned to speak.

He skimmed it, a smile spreading across his face. "This is good. This is very good."

She nodded slowly, still processing the gravity of the moment. "Do you think she actually... likes me?"

He shrugged. "I think she respects you. And in her world, that's much more important."

The day of the tea arrived, and she stood once again before the mirror, feeling out of place in the elegant dress she had chosen for the occasion.

That time, there was a flicker of confidence in her reflection because she had survived the gala, and she would survive this too.

The carriage ride to the Baroness's estate was filled with nervous energy. He had wanted to come with her, but she had insisted on going alone. This was her battle to fight.

When she arrived at the grand estate, she was greeted by the Baroness herself, a striking woman in her fifties with sharp eyes and a graceful demeanor. They exchanged pleasantries as they walked through the lush garden, the atmosphere surprisingly relaxed.

As they sat down for tea, the Baroness studied her for a moment before speaking. "You know, I've seen many women try to navigate our world... most of them fail."

She met the Baroness's gaze, her heart pounding in her chest. "I don't plan on failing."

The Baroness smiled, a glint of approval in her eyes. "Good. I didn't think you would."

The conversation flowed easily after that; the Baroness asking questions about her past, her relationship, and her thoughts on society.

It was clear the woman was testing her, but she held her ground, answering each question with honesty and grace.

As the tea ended, the Baroness stood and offered her hand. "I believe you'll do just fine in our world," she said, her tone warm. "And I look forward to seeing you at the next event."

It wasn't a grand declaration of acceptance, but it was something akin to a minor victory, a step toward belonging. As she left the estate, she felt a sense of accomplishment. The Baroness's approval, however subtle, was a sign that the tides were turn**ing.**

Over the next few weeks, she noticed slight changes in the way people treated her. The whispers behind her back grew quieter, the stares less hostile. People nodded in greeting when they saw her, some even engaging her in polite conversation.

There were still some who doubted her, but cracks were appearing in their closed-mindedness. And with each crack, her confidence grew.

One evening, as they sat together on the veranda, he took her hand in his, his thumb gently brushing against her skin. "I told you things would get better."

She smiled, resting her head against his shoulder. "I didn't believe you."

He chuckled softly. "You should start believing in yourself more. You're stronger than you know."

She closed her eyes, feeling the warmth of his presence beside her. "Maybe I am."

CHAPTER-26

*A*s the weeks passed, the subtle shifts in how society treated her brought new challenges.

The whispers might have quieted, but beneath the surface, resentment brewed among those who couldn't accept her rise.

For every approving glance, there were still eyes watching, waiting for her to falter. The air inside the grand house felt heavier with each passing day.

It wasn't long before that resentment took form.

One afternoon, she was busy in the kitchen, helping one of the maids with some simple chores, when a loud knock echoed through the halls. The maid stiffened, glancing nervously toward the front of the house.

"I'll get it," she said, drying her hands on her apron and heading to the door. When she opened it, she was greeted by the sight of two men, one she recognized as a local sheriff, the other a figure from her past.

Her blood ran cold as the second man stepped forward, his eyes narrowing in recognition.

It had been years since she'd seen him, but the memories flooded back instantly. He was a bounty hunter, the same man who had once tried to capture her when she was on the run.

"Well, well," he drawled, his voice low and menacing. "Looks like I've finally found you."

She took a step back, her heart hammering in her chest. "I don't know what you're talking about."

"Don't play games," he snapped. "You think just because you've landed yourself in this fancy house, you can outrun your past? You still owe me."

Her breath caught in her throat as the sheriff stepped forward, holding up a document. "There's a warrant for your arrest," he said grimly. "For theft."

She felt the ground beneath her shift, her carefully constructed world beginning to crack. "This is a mistake," she said, her voice trembling slightly. "I have stolen nothing."

"Not recently, maybe," the bounty hunter sneered. "But I remember you, girl. You were running from town to town, stealing whatever you could. You've been lucky so far, but your luck's run out."

Her mind raced as she tried to think of a way out, but before she could speak again, Lucien appeared. He had heard the commotion and entered the hall, his eyes immediately locking onto the men at the door.

"What's going on here?" he demanded, his voice commanding and cold.

The sheriff cleared his throat. "We believe this woman is wanted for theft. We have a warrant."

He stepped in front of her, shielding her from their view. "You will not touch her," he said, his tone leaving no room for argument. "There's been a misunderstanding."

The bounty hunter snorted. "Misunderstanding or not, the law is the law."

His jaw clenched, but he didn't waver. "How much?" he asked, his voice low.

"What?"

"How much is the bounty?"

The bounty hunter's eyes gleamed with greed. "Twenty gold pieces."

Without a second thought, he reached into his coat, pulling out a small leather pouch. He tossed it at the bounty hunter's feet. "There's your money. Now leave."

As the men left, she stood frozen, her mind swirling with emotions she couldn't quite process. Relief, fear, shame, all mixing in a tumultuous storm. He turned to her, his face softening as he reached for her hand.

"Are you alright?"

She pulled back, her heart still racing. "You paid them off. Just like that."

He frowned, clearly not understanding her reaction. "I did what I had to do. I will not let them take you."

"But you just paid them like I was... like I was something to be bought."

His eyes widened in surprise. "That's not what I meant—"

"You don't understand," she interrupted, her voice rising. "I'd been running my whole life, fighting to survive. I felt like I was back at square one, like none of this means anything if someone can just walk in here and take me away."

He stepped closer, his voice gentle but firm. "The person you were back then is not the same as who you are now. You're different now, grown."

"But I'm still not free," she whispered, her eyes filling with tears. "And no matter what we do, there will always be people like them who see me as nothing more than a criminal."

He reached out, taking her hand in his. "It gets better," he promised.

It wasn't just the bounty hunter or the sheriff that haunted her. The actual battle was within her because, for so long, she had fought to survive on her own terms, never relying on anyone else.

Now, she faced the reality that her past could always come back to claim her, no matter how far she had come.

Over the following days, the tension between them grew. She couldn't shake the feeling that she had lost control of her life once again, that her freedom was slipping away.

What if more of her past victims came forward? Who knew how hard their enemies were plotting to have her past come back to haunt her, and what was coming next?

He tried to reassure her, to remind her they were in it together, but the walls she had built over the years were hard to break down. He knew that it was necessary for her to overcome that fear on her own.

CHAPTER-27

*A*s the first rays of dawn peeked through the curtains, she stirred beneath the covers, blinking awake to the peaceful chirp of birds outside her window.

For a moment, she lay still, feeling the quiet wash over her, a stark contrast to the tension that had gripped her heart just days ago.

The events with the sheriff and bounty hunter still echoed in her mind, but they no longer held the same power.

Instead, there was a calm that settled over her, as if the storm had finally passed. Her hand instinctively reached out to his side of the bed, but the sheets were cool, meaning he'd been up for hours, no doubt tending to his endless duties.

She rose and dressed, slipping into a simple gown that was feeling more familiar than foreign. As she descended the grand staircase, she listened for the steady rhythm of his footsteps. Instead, the house was still, save for the occasional crackle of the fireplace in the distant parlor.

It was in the study she found him, sitting behind his desk, his brow furrowed as he pored over stacks of papers. The sight of him, so composed, so focused, made her heart clench.

She hesitated in the doorway, watching him for a beat longer than usual, a soft smile tugging at her lips. He was everything she never thought she'd need.

When he finally looked up, his face softened instantly. "Good morning," he said, his voice warm and inviting, as if they were the only two people in the world.

"Morning," she replied, stepping into the room. She settled into the chair opposite him, studying his face, the lines of concentration still etched across his brow. "You're already hard at work."

He leaned back in his chair, setting the papers aside with a sigh. "There's always something that needs tending to around here," he admitted. "But today... I'm thinking I'll let it all wait."

Her brows lifted in surprise. "You? Take a break?" she teased, folding her arms. "Isn't that sacrilege in your world?"

A playful smile tugged at his lips as he stood, walking over to her side. "I think we've earned it, don't you?" He held out his hand. "Let's spend the day together. No distractions. Just us."

The air outside was crisp and cool, with the faint scent of earth and leaves lingering in the breeze. As they walked hand in hand through the orchard, she marveled at the serenity.

For so long, her life had been one of chaos, of survival, never knowing where her next meal would come from or if she'd live to see the next day. Now, here she was, strolling through a sea of apple trees with a man who had seen past her rough edges, who had chosen her.

She caught him watching her out of the corner of her eye, a contemplative look on his face.

"What?" she asked, her tone light but curious.

He shrugged, his smile deepening. "You're just... different out here. I enjoy seeing you like this. At peace."

Her steps faltered for a moment, and she turned to face him fully. "Peace?" She laughed softly, shaking her head. "I didn't think I would ever know peace."

"Yet here it is," he said, his voice steady.

They continued their walk, talking about small things, the orchard, the estate, the way the leaves shimmered in the light of the setting sun. Things had improved vastly since her tea with the Baroness and business had vastly improved.

As they wandered back toward the house, the conversation shifted and she spoke about her dreams, her voice tentative at first, as if afraid to give life to them.

"I've been thinking," she started, glancing at him, "about what I might want to do... in the future."

He arched a brow. "Oh? And what might that be?"

She hesitated, feeling a rush of vulnerability. "I... I want to open a school. For girls. For women like me, who never had the chance to learn, to grow."

His expression softened, and he stopped walking, turning to face her. "A school?"

She nodded, her heart pounding. "Yes. A place where they can come and be taught, where they don't have to be afraid of what the world might do to them. I want to help them find their place, just like I'm finding mine."

For a long moment, he said nothing, simply staring at her, a deep emotion simmering in his gaze. Then, without warning, he pulled her into his arms, holding her close.

"I think that's a brilliant idea," he murmured against her hair. "And I'll help you. Whatever you need, we'll make it happen."

She blinked back the tears that suddenly pricked at her eyes, overwhelmed by the magnitude of his support. "You really mean that?"

He cupped her face in his hands, his thumb gently brushing her cheek. "Of course I do. You're not just building your life anymore, woman. We're building it together."

Later that evening, after a simple dinner shared in quiet companionship, they sat together in the parlor while the fire crackled softly in the hearth. She sipped her tea, her body finally feeling at ease for the first time in what seemed like forever.

He, however, seemed restless. She could see it in the way his leg bounced slightly, in the way he kept glancing her way as if he had something to say.

"Is something on your mind?" she asked, setting her cup down and watching him intently.

He met her gaze, and for a moment, there was a flicker of hesitation in his eyes, something rare for him. Then he stood, reaching into his pocket as he took a deep breath. "Actually, yes."

Her heart pounded, her instincts telling her that something significant was about to happen. She sat up straighter, her eyes locked on him as he pulled out a small velvet box, his fingers tightening around it as if it carried the value of the world.

He approached her, kneeling before her in one smooth motion, his eyes never leaving hers.

"I've been thinking about us," he began, his voice softer now, filled with an emotion she had rarely heard from him. "And about what you said earlier, about your dreams, about our future."

Her breath caught in her throat, the room suddenly feeling too small, too charged.

"I don't just want you here as my companion, or as someone to pass the time with. I want you to be my partner and for us to build this life together, for real." He opened the box, revealing a simple yet elegant ring. "Marry me."

For a moment, the world seemed to stand still. The embers crackled softly in the background, but all she could hear was the pounding of her own heartbeat. She stared at the ring, her mind racing with a thousand thoughts.

Marriage. A life. With him.

The woman she had been before, wild, untamed, crude, would have scoffed at such an idea. But now, standing on the edge of something new, something good, she realized she wanted it. She wanted him.

Tears welled up in her eyes, and she nodded, unable to speak. "Yes," she whispered, her voice thick with emotion. "Yes, I'll marry you."

He smiled widely and gently put the ring on her finger, pulling her into a warm embrace as they laughed and cried tears of joy together.

They stayed like that for a long time, wrapped in each other's warmth.

EPILOGUE

SIX YEARS LATER

*W*ith its warm glow, the morning sun enveloped the house, illuminating the hallways, and filling the rooms with life.

The once-quiet estate now buzzed with the sound of children's laughter, the pitter-patter of small feet echoing throughout.

The faint smell of fresh bread wafted from the kitchen, mingling with the earthy scent of the gardens just beyond the veranda.

She stood at the window of the sitting room, looking out over the land that had become her home. The fields stretched out toward the horizon, a sea of green that rolled in waves with the wind. She could hear the workers outside tending to the crops, and for the first time in years, there was peace.

The small, simple gold band on her finger glinted in the sunlight, a reminder of the day that had changed everything. Their wedding had been modest, attended by only a handful of trusted friends and workers.

It had been enough, more than enough. The vows they had exchanged under the shade of the old oak tree in the garden were etched into her memory, promises made not just to each other, but to the life they were building together.

It hadn't been easy, and the world around them hadn't softened overnight. She was still viewed by many with disdain, her very presence in his life an affront to their rigid societal norms.

Things were changing, slowly, subtly. There was a truce now, an unspoken agreement between them and the town. She wasn't accepted, not fully, but she was no longer a target and that was enough.

His business, once teetering on the edge, thrived again. The whispers that had circled around him for taking her in as his wife had faded into the background, replaced by admiration for his tenacity and vision.

He had built something strong, something that weathered the storms of public opinion. And she, well... she had found her own way to thrive, too.

The school was her pride and joy. Nestled at the edge of their estate, it was small, but full of promise. She had started with just a few children from the nearby community, those who had no other place to learn and had been forgotten by the larger towns and plantations.

Now, it had grown into something far greater, a beacon of hope for those seeking an education in a world that had often denied it to them.

From her vantage point by the window, she watched as the children engaged in play during recess, their infectious laughter resonating throughout the surroundings.

The sight filled her heart with pride. She had created something lasting, something that would outlive her, just as her husband had done with his business. Together, they had built a legacy.

A sudden crash echoed from the hallway, followed by a loud, childish giggle. She turned just in time to see the twins, two lively boys with dark curls and bright eyes, tumble into the room. They were a whirlwind of energy, their laughter infectious as they skidded to a stop in front of her, their tiny faces flushed from running.

"Mama!" one of them cried, holding up a small wooden horse, clearly proud of some new discovery. "Look what we found!"

She crouched down, her heart swelling as she took the toy from his hands. "It's a fine horse," she said, her voice soft with affection. "But where did you get it?"

The other twin, not to be outdone, tugged at her dress. "We found it in Daddy's study!"

Before she could respond, a familiar voice interrupted from the doorway. "Now, what have I told you two about going into my study without asking?"

Her husband's voice was playful, but there was a hint of mock seriousness in it. He leaned against the doorframe, arms crossed over his chest, his lips curling into a smile as he watched their sons.

The boys, unfazed by his mild rebuke, launched themselves at him, their little arms wrapping around his legs. He scooped them up effortlessly, a laugh rumbling from his chest as they clung to him.

She watched the scene unfold, her heart so full it felt like it might burst. This was her life now, this bustling, chaotic, beautiful life. It was more than she had ever dared dream of when she was just a woman trying to survive, singing in bars, and stealing to get by. And now, here she was, a mother, a wife, and a lady.

"I see recess is winding down, so you'd better go join your fellow students," she said as the kids ran towards the door.

That evening, they sat together on the veranda. The boys had long since been put to bed, their small bodies worn out from a day of play. The house was quiet now, save for the occasional sound of the wind rustling through the trees.

She leaned her head against his shoulder, her hand resting on his chest, feeling the steady rhythm of his heartbeat beneath her fingers.

"We've come a long way," he murmured, his lips brushing the top of her head.

She smiled, closing her eyes as she let the peace of the moment wash over her. "Yes, we have."

There was a long silence between them, comfortable and familiar, before he spoke again.

"Do you ever think about that day?" he asked quietly. "When we met?"

She laughed softly, lifting her head to look at him. "How could I forget? You thought I was trying to steal from you."

"And you were," he teased, his eyes twinkling with amusement.

She smiled, leaning in to kiss him gently. "Maybe. But if I hadn't, we wouldn't be here now, would we?"

"No," he agreed, his voice soft with affection. "We wouldn't."

They sat like that for a while longer, watching the sky darken, the stars beginning to appear one by one. The world had changed around them, but in that moment, it was just the two of them, together, as they always had been.

As the night deepened, she let out a contented sigh. There were still challenges ahead, still battles to be fought.

They had made it this far and would continue to persevere.

XOXO

Join my newsletter to stay informed about new releases.

THANK YOU

Thank you for your purchase. You can sign up to my mailing list to receive notification whenever a new book releases.

If you enjoyed it, I would appreciate a customer review.

Join here: or scan with your phone:

A forbidden love, a dangerous escape, a future worth fighting for.

Love is a dangerous rebellion in a world where freedom is a distant dream.

Elara has known only chains and fear since being captured and sold to a brutal plantation owner. But the one bright spot in her life had always been Nathaniel, the master's son who, even as a boy, dared to look at her differently. They shared forbidden moments beneath the oak trees, stolen glances that grew into something deeper, more dangerous.

Years have passed since Nathaniel was sent away, and Elara

thought their connection was lost forever. But now he's back, hardened, determined, and ready to risk everything to free her from the life that has bound her for too long.

As they flee through the wilderness, hunted by those who would see them both dead, their past collides with their desperate present. The fire between them burns brighter as their bond strengthens. Danger lurks behind every tree, and both know the cost of their passion could be fatal.

Can they outrun the shackles of a world that forbids their love, or will they be forced to pay the ultimate price for their defiance?

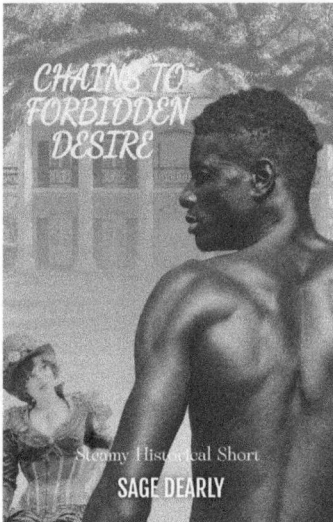

In the heart of the antebellum South, Kwame, a newly arrived slave to the sprawling southern plantation, finds himself thrust into a delicate dance of desire and power.

Caught in the gaze of the lady of the house, he is swiftly reassigned to her quarters, a shift that promises opportunity.

When the master of the plantation is away, he leaves the vast estate momentarily unguarded and the lady seizes her chance.

Amidst the flickering flames of forbidden passion, another presence lingers—the lady's daughter, a young woman torn between curiosity and jealousy as she watches their clandestine affair unfold.

For Kwame, the allure of female companionship is a beacon of solace in the oppressive shadows of servitude, igniting a fire within him that drives him to navigate the treacherous waters of plantation life with cunning and determination.

Find the series at my store.

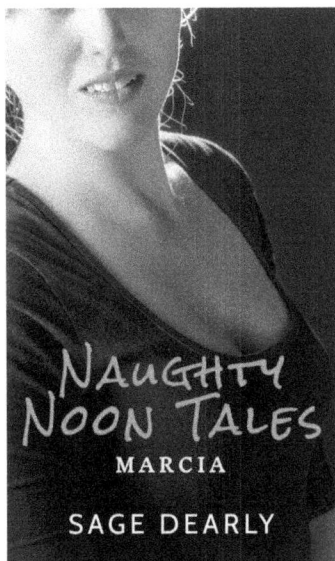

NAUGHTY NOON TALES

MARCIA

SAGE DEARLY

Naughty Noon Tales: Marcia

Marcia is a lonely and restless housewife whose mundane world takes an unexpected turn in the intoxicating heat of "Naughty Noon Tales."

When a substitute gardener tends to more than just her garden, she finds herself entangled in a web of desire and forbidden passion.

The clock ticks towards noon and Marcia succumbs to a liaison that is quite different from her predictable life.

In the sultry haze of midday, Marcia's confession unfolds. You don't want to miss this seductive confession.

Find the series at the store.

Vaneeta's life at the plantation is about to change when she meets the plantation owner's twin brother who's there to celebrate their birthday.

Amid all the preparations, she is eager to give them her special present. An exceptional night for the threesome and there was no going back once she experienced the exquisite pleasure of the flesh.

Her life lesson continues when the other brothers come to visit and partake in the sexual awakening in the sequential books that can be read as stand-alone also.

Buy Them Here

You can also find Sage Dearly books on your favorite online platforms.

ABOUT THE AUTHOR

Sage Dearly is an emerging author of romance that runs the gamut from clean to smutty. All her historical shorts are light on the history.

She has dreamt of writing since she was a youngster when she accidentally happened upon sexually explicit books at a bookstore.

Now, she's finally living that dream and loving it. You can support her by buying direct on her website and subscribing to the newsletter.

Sage's website

9 798227 705990